Hart & Soal

Protectors, Volume 2

Kit Kyndall

Published by Amourisa Press, 2017.

Blurb

After his injuries forced U.S. Marshal Andre Hart to retire, an old friend recruits him to do security for a reality TV star plastic surgeon with a stalker. One look at Dr. Shannon Soal, and he's hooked. She requests he pose as her lover to hide her stalker problem and increased need for security from the public. Though unorthodox, that's no sacrifice. The only problem is keeping it a pretense instead of making it a reality. They fight their attraction, but how can they deny their hearts when they might have found their soulmates?

Meanwhile, Shannon's stalker has death in mind and won't give up on her easily. Or ever.

Andre Hart first appeared in "Safe Harbor." This story is a standalone, but you might enjoy seeing Andre in that story.

Chapter One

DR. SHANNON SOAL CAREFULLY closed the incision on Mrs. Bailey's stomach, barely aware of the cameras in the room. During the last eighteen months that her practice had participated in the reality show, the cameras had become commonplace. She operated just as she always did, with her sole focus on her patient, and not remembering that she was part of a TV show until after she stepped out of the operating theater.

She moved away from her patient, heading toward the scrub sink. After stripping her gloves, she scrubbed thoroughly and grabbed a towel. As she moved through the scrub room, she briefly remembered the producer liked her to remove her cap as she exited. Angus Calvin claimed it made her look more approachable, but she suspected it had more to do with the fact her beautiful dark hair would increase her physical appeal. She left the cap on, too tired to bother with removing it and pandering to the producer that day.

She made her way down the hall to find Mrs. Bailey's family. They had agreed to allow the film crew in with them while they waited for news about their wife and mother. She tried not to be cynical, but she hadn't been surprised. People almost always allowed themselves to be persuaded into being featured on the show. It was only natural, she supposed, to want to have one's fifteen minutes of fame, and she doubted the people who appeared briefly on the show give it much thought beyond that.

She had ensured there was a clause in the contract the family signed that if she had to deliver bad news—something that had happened on three occasions during the last eighteen months—the camera crews would immediately stop filming, and nothing would be included in the show. Angus hadn't liked it, but it was one of Shannon's stipulations for participating when her two partners had discussed the idea with her after Med TV made the offer to them.

Thankfully, she had good news to deliver to the balding, punchy husband and the teen-to-young-adult children waiting. "Mrs. Bailey's liposuction procedure was flawless. She'll be in recovery for a short time, and then you can see her."

"Will there be any complications, Dr. Soal?" asked Saul...no, Sal Bailey.

Shannon found a smile for him, and she hoped it was reassuring. She couldn't let her lousy day make the family worry by accidentally transmitting a concern she didn't have for Stella Bailey. "I don't anticipate any problems at all. Everything went smoothly, and your wife is in excellent health." The older woman had been a scant twenty pounds overweight, and while Shannon understood why Mrs. Bailey wanted to shed the weight, it wasn't something for which she herself would've had surgery.

A lot of the operations she conducted were like that—tummy sculpting, breast enhancement, and rhinoplasty. It was those cases, and the often exorbitant fees attached to them due to her practice's prestige, that allowed her to fund her true passion, so she operated whenever it was feasible if it made someone happy, because ultimately it would make more than one person happy. It funded her foundation, which provided free operations for people suffering from deformities, burns, and other disfiguring conditions that might be alleviated, if not completely cured, under the skillful application of her scalpel.

After leaving the family waiting room, she stepped into the hallway and found Matt, one of the camera guys, waiting for her with the camera on his shoulder. This part was expected, but she was suddenly weary. Somehow, she forced a smile for the camera and gave a quick wrap-up of the case. She truly expected no complications for Mrs. Bailey and likely wouldn't see the woman again until her post-operative appointment at the office. That too would be filmed, but probably wouldn't make the cut for the week's episode unless there was some drama to the case.

After that, she was finally freed from her obligations to her patient and the show for the time being. She walked down the halls of the outpatient surgical center owned by her practice and into her office.

It was technically a dressing room, complete with a makeup station and wardrobe. There were myriad scrubs available to her, and she could pick whatever caught her fancy that day. Other than having someone do her makeup and pin her hair under her cap, she was fairly independent with all the other aspects of her appearance on the show. Today, she had chosen black scrubs to match her mood.

She collapsed on the sofa and stretched out as she tried to summon the energy to move from her office/dressing room at the surgical center to her real office in the building across the parking lot. She shouldn't be so drained, since she'd only had two surgeries that morning, and she had a blissful ninety minutes to rest before her first appointment at the clinic. She knew what was bothering her, what had left her enervated, and what made crossing the parking lot such a daunting task.

Your crocs didn't match your scrubs yesterday, Dr. Soal.

Shannon didn't have to walk over to the table where she'd set the note to remember the words. It wasn't the first strange note she'd received since starting to participate in the reality show, but they had become more frequent of late, and clearly from the same person. She still received other fan mail, along with at least a dozen marriage proposals and other less savory proposals from diehard fans each week, but those were just somewhere between mildly amusing and downright disgusting. They didn't leave her with the creepy, watched feeling that was settling over her again.

She wished she hadn't opened it before starting surgery that morning, because it had been haunting her throughout the day. In one way, Shannon wished she hadn't opened it at all, but it was better to know. Someone was watching her. Genuinely, literally watching her.

For one thing, she knew the person was referring to yesterday, because it was the first time she'd worn her new pair of crocs. The shows were taped live, but edited and not actually shown on the network for anywhere from two to four weeks, depending on the cases and the people involved. That eliminated the possibility that someone had seen her crocs on television, which would have been unlikely anyway, since filming was usually above the waist or centered on the surgical table.

For another, she had worn her reliable sneakers during surgery yesterday. They were the same pair gracing her feet now, and she kicked them off without thought. They were kept strictly for use in the surgical center and weren't outside shoes. Her new crocs waited for her feet to slide into them, but she made no move to do so.

She should be stirring around and getting lunch before preparing for a busy afternoon of meeting with patients, but instead, she was hiding in her dressing room because it felt safe. If someone was watching her and had watched her make the trek from the surgical center to their office yesterday, they would probably be watching again today.

It was disquieting, and she reached for the cell phone she'd left on the table by the couch. She dialed the number from memory, having spoken with Detective Jared Silver many times over the past few weeks, following his directions to contact him each time she received a new letter. She had been resistant to the idea of filing a police report to start with, but her assistant and best friend, Misty, had interceded and called in the detective without her permission.

Today, she was glad Misty had been so proactive, because what had once seemed ridiculous and harmless now felt vaguely threatening. "Hello, Detective Silver. This is Shannon Soal."

"I recognized your voice, Dr. Soal. And your phone number." There was a hint of flirtation in his tone, and he'd made no secret of the fact that he would like to get to know her better in a nonprofessional capacity. "What can I do for you today? Another letter?"

"Yes, and this one's worse than the others." She quickly detailed what had bothered her about it, and when he spoke again, he was all business.

"If someone is watching you, you need to increase your security."

"We've already hired more people to do patrols."

The detective let out a small sigh. "That's not what I mean, and you know it, Dr. Soal. You promised me that if things escalated, you would get private security. You know I can't be available twenty-four/seven unless there's a true threat, and we don't want it to escalate to that point."

She sighed. "But a bodyguard will suck the last of my privacy away. I really don't want someone following me around, hovering, and playing Kevin Costner to my Whitney Houston."

The detective chuckled. "I don't think you have anything to worry about, Dr. Soal. I saw the Christmas party episode, where you got tipsy and performed karaoke. You're no Whitney Houston."

She rolled her eyes, but a small giggle escaped her. "Touché. But do you understand my objections?"

The detective hesitated for a moment. "Of course I understand not wanting to give up your privacy, but do you understand my concern? You need someone there who's available immediately if needed. It could take minutes or longer for dispatch to send help if you need it. You have my private cell phone number, but I live thirty minutes away in typical L.A. traffic. This is your safety we're talking about. Which is more important—your safety or your privacy?"

She winced. "Low blow, Detective Silver."

He sounded unapologetic. "I have some people I can refer you to—"

"No people. A person. Maybe." Shannon closed her eyes for a minute before exhaling. "There has to be a way to do this that's discreet.

I don't want my possible stalker situation to turn into more drama for the television show. If different people are following me around and changing out every few hours, it's going to be awkward to explain."

"I might have an idea for you. May I call you back in a few minutes after I speak with someone?"

She nodded before remembering he couldn't see her through the phone. "Of course. I'll still be here." She had no intention of leaving her dressing room until she absolutely had to.

After hanging up, she got up from the sofa and moved to the small refrigerator, where she kept snacks on the days she ran late. She raided her refrigerator for a quick, healthy lunch before returning to the couch, this time sitting up instead of lying down.

It seemed to take forever for the phone to ring, and she quickly set aside the container of fruit she'd munched on when it rang. She looked at the screen long enough to confirm it was Detective Silver before answering. "Hello?"

"I have a friend named Andre Hart. He used to be a U.S. Marshal, but he was seriously wounded several months ago. He was forced to retire from the Marshals, and he's been doing some light security work since then. He's agreeable to being your only security for a time, though he wishes that you would add more people to the team. I wish the same."

"One's bad enough. How badly was he injured?" She felt bad asking the question, but she had to be sure that if she accepted a bodyguard, he could actually protect her if the need arose.

"He's doing much better now, and I wouldn't entrust your safety to him if he wasn't able to see to it. Should I send him over?"

Shannon hesitated. "I still don't understand how it's going to work. How do I explain him?"

The detective laughed. "You could pretend he's your boyfriend. There wouldn't be much question about him appearing at your side, especially since you're a beautiful woman, and any man lucky enough to be your lover would want to be beside you as much as possible."

She shivered at the intimate tone in his voice, nonplussed by the indication that his attraction had only grown stronger. There was nothing wrong with the detective per se, but she wasn't in a place where she wanted to pursue a relationship, especially with the man coordinating the investigation into her stalking.

It felt so melodramatic to call it that, and she still mostly believed it would turn out to be a harmless, though probably emotionally unstable, fan with too much devotion. Still, she didn't want to risk muddying the investigation when she wasn't attracted to the detective. "I guess you could send him over, and we can at least talk about the idea."

"Good girl," he said in a way that he probably didn't mean to sound condescending, but came across that way. "I'll send Andre to you. Where would you like to meet him?"

For a moment, she was tempted to blurt out the surgical center, not wanting to make the walk across the parking lot on her own. Knowing she lacked sufficient time to have a proper meeting with him quelled the urge. Instead, she said, "If it's agreeable to him, have him meet me at my condo tonight at seven, please. The address is—"

"I have the address," said the detective. "It's in your police report."

"Of course. Thank you, Detective Silver."

"You're welcome, Shannon." He said her name in a too-familiar tone.

She didn't bother to call him on it as she hung up without speaking again. The detective's attraction was just something else she'd have to deal with on her already too-full plate. He paled in comparison to her current worries, chief among them that some unhinged person was watching her every move and thinking about her obsessively. She hoped she'd just watched too much TV, and even clung to the idea that the Andre Hart she was meeting that night would reassure her that her fears were unfounded and tell her she didn't need him after all.

After finishing her lunch, she slipped her feet into the crocs and walked out of her dressing room. Less than a minute later, she was at the door leading to the parking lot, and she hesitated. She couldn't bring herself to step out alone, so she started to turn to look for a security guard to escort her when the door opened from the outside, and Misty stepped in. A wave of relief at the sight of her blonde-haired friend swept through her, and she smiled. "What are you doing here?" Misty rarely ventured into the surgical center, telling Shannon once that the antiseptic smells and the knowledge of what went on there gave her bad memories. Shannon didn't know memories of what, but she sympathized.

"You're running late, and I wanted to check on you."

Shannon smiled. "I appreciate that. I know how difficult it is for you to come to the surgical center." She glanced at her watch. "I'm not really running late though, am I?"

Misty shrugged. "Not terribly so, but you usually come to your office straight after you finish filming for the day, and that's usually over with by twelve-thirty. It's closer to two now, and you have an appointment in fifteen minutes."

Shannon nodded, stepping out of the surgical center and walking with Misty across the parking lot. It was still unnerving, and she was certain she could feel eyes upon her, but she was bolstered by her friend's presence. "Thanks for keeping me on track, Misty."

Her assistant bumped her arm. "That's my job, and what are friends for?"

"I'm glad to have a friend like you." Living in L.A. as somewhat of a minor celebrity, Shannon had lots of acquaintances, but very few people to whom she felt genuinely close. While both of her partners seemed to have embraced the reality TV star lifestyle, Shannon was still having some difficulty with it even eighteen months after the hoopla had begun.

If it weren't for the hefty payout, which went directly to funding her foundation, she would have refused to participate. That would have been practically impossible in their three-doctor practice, so she would have had to leave the practice as well.

She'd made the best decision she could, and now she had to live with it, though she disliked many aspects of the lifestyle. At least she had close friends like Misty, who she'd only known for little more than a year, but had become like a sister to her. She was thankful she had chosen Misty's application and résumé from the pile submitted to act as her assistant when her previous office manager had decided to retire after the show started shooting. It had been too much for Mabel, who had only been a few scant years away from retirement anyway.

Misty had been a lucky find, and she hoped her luck continued when she met with the bodyguard that night. If he couldn't reassure her that she didn't need him, she hoped she could at least become friends with him, especially if they were going to go through some kind of elaborate pretense, pretending to be a couple.

Chapter Two

WITHIN FIVE MINUTES of meeting Andre Hart, Shannon wasn't entirely certain how much it would be pretend. He sat stiffly on her white sofa, having shown up promptly at seven at her condo's entryway to be buzzed in. Watching him discreetly, she suspected the way he sat had more to do with some lingering pain from his injury than that he was awkward in her presence. He seemed completely relaxed around her, though there was an air of watchful vigilance around him that was soothing and reassuring.

She held out the lemonade he'd requested before sitting down in a chair beside the sofa. As she took a sip of her own, she eyed him from the corner of her eye, her mouth going dry despite the drink she had just ingested.

He was handsome. Andre was taller than her, which was rare, and broad through the shoulders, with a narrow waist. He had closely-cropped black hair that tamed its natural curl, and his skin was a shade of that pricey dark chocolate she sometimes allowed to make its way into her cart when she was at Trader Joe's.

When she had the disquieting urge to lean forward and lick him, to find out if he was as bittersweet as her favorite chocolate, she immediately looked away and took a huge gulp of her lemonade to distract herself.

Her thoughts were inappropriate. If she didn't want to get involved with the detective investigating her case, for fear of it muddying his focus, she certainly should avoid any sort of entanglement with the person who might act as her bodyguard on a twenty-four/seven basis. He would be far more intimately involved in her life than the detective.

She almost groaned aloud when her mind supplied several images of him being very intimately connected to her life. She closed her eyes for a moment and took a deep breath before opening them and forcing herself to stop behaving like a ninny and look at Andre Hart. "Thank you for coming, Mr. Hart."

"Of course. I know Jared from my days as a U.S. Marshal. He told me what you're up against, but I'd like to hear it from you."

She took a deep breath before she started telling Andre about the situation. "The notes started out innocuously enough. They weren't at all threatening, and they were flattering. I didn't think much of them to start with, but then they started changing."

He had flipped open an old-fashioned notebook and was taking notes with a pen. "How did they change?"

"They started to become more personal, along with not exactly outright insults, but...gaslighting, maybe? There were backhanded compliments like, 'Your makeup artist really knows how to hide the shadows under your eyes.' Just little things that were enough to catch my attention and make me uncomfortable."

"Do you still have them?"

Shannon got up, smoothing her palazzo pants as she moved to the writing desk in the corner to lift the lid and retrieve the bag of notes she kept there. "I have most of them. Jared took a few to check for fingerprints, and I believe he admitted them as evidence. He actually took the whole pile, but returned these."

Andre looked puzzled. "Did you want them back?"

Shannon hesitated before nodding. A touch of embarrassment filled her, and her cheeks turned warm. "Yes."

His frown deepened, and his mahogany eyes were filled with confusion. "Why would you want those?"

She shrugged a shoulder. "I can't really put it into words exactly, but in a way, having them makes me feel better. Not the words themselves, but the fact that they exist. If I'm doubting whether I'm overreacting, just a quick glimpse of them reminds me that I'm probably not. If I feel threatened, I probably am. Does that make sense?"

He nodded. "You aren't rereading them though?" The question was asked casually, but his concern was obvious.

Shannon laughed. "No, I'm not rereading them. I haven't even looked at them since Detective Silver returned them to me. I've just been adding the new letters as they come."

"And the detective hasn't examined them again?"

"I've arranged for him to pick them up once a week." She was certain Detective Silver would have happily come by to get them every day if she would allow it, but having that much more exposure to the detective had seemed like a bad idea when she wanted to discourage his interest. "I can send them along with you if you're going to see him soon?"

"I think that can be arranged. I'm particularly interested in the newest one. He mentioned your stalker is escalating?"

Shannon shrugged, and the open neckline of her loose shirt slipped down her shoulder. She didn't miss the way his gaze followed the movement as she shrugged it back up. There was definitely a spark of interest there, and it filled her with dread. Not like she dreaded having to deal with another situation like the detective's unwanted attraction. This was more a sense of dread that her interest mirrored his, and it was going to be difficult, if not impossible, to resist his allure. "I'm not sure I would call him a stalker." She handed over the packet of notes to which she had added the most recent one on top upon arriving home. "That sounds so overly dramatic."

"It's better to regard it with an overabundance of caution than to be careless and disregard a threat."

Shannon nodded her agreement at his words and waited while he read through the latest letter, viewing it through the plastic. His lips were pursed as he read, and she had the crazy urge to lean forward and smooth them out with her thumb.

"That definitely sounds slightly menacing, especially when combined with what Jared told me." His expression was completely businesslike when he met her gaze. "I think Jared's right, and you should have full-time protection. I'm a one-person operation at the moment, just doing some part-time security work, along with some discreet investigating. I know some people who run a firm, and they'll take good care of you—"

Shannon held up her hand to interrupt him. "No, thanks. I don't want a full security detail if I can avoid it. Didn't Jared mention that to you?" It was the first time she'd called the detective by his first name, and it felt wrong in her mouth.

"He did, but I was hoping to talk you into choosing a more sensible course. I'll be happy to protect you, but I'm just one person. I have to sleep sometimes."

The flare of heat in his eyes made her press her thighs together, and she had little doubt that he was thinking about something else besides sleeping just then. "I'd still rather avoid the whole dog-and-pony show of having multiple bodyguards. I'm under enough scrutiny as it is, and I don't need extra gossip. There'll be people gossiping about my stalker, and then there'll be people calling me a liar and saying I'm doing it for attention. I'd rather just keep it low-key with you. The detective mentioned something about a phony relationship context?" She tried to be subtle with the question as she wrapped a strand of dark hair around her fingers, feeling unaccountably nervous, as though she was actually interviewing Andre as a boyfriend rather than as a bodyguard.

"It would work if you're determined to just have one person. It makes sense to have that person pose as someone close to you. If you're sure that's what you want, I'll take care of you."

She had to squeeze her thighs together tighter as she imagined him taking care of her in a completely different way. It was probably a bad idea to hire him, with the raging attraction between them, but she couldn't imagine pretending to be involved with someone else. Until meeting Andre, she hadn't thought she could do it anyway, but now it felt like it would be surprisingly easy to pretend to be a couple. Too easy, and the pretense could quickly become real. "I'd appreciate your help. How does this work?"

"I can move in tonight, if you'd like, or we can wait until morning?"

She licked her lips. "What do you think I should do?"

He seemed unabashed when he said, "I brought some things with me, and they're in my car in the parking garage. I think you should have protection as soon as possible."

She had plenty of protection. Refusing to allow her thoughts to remain on the box of condoms in her nightstand, she kept her expression as placid as possible to avoid revealing the wayward direction of her thoughts. "In that case, I'll show you where the guest room is, and you can get settled in."

He nodded brusquely as he stood up, waiting for her to lead him. She fell into step before him and took him down the hallway. Her condo was on the small side, but it had two bedrooms, and she showed him to the guest room. "I hope it will do for you. It's a little small."

Andre laughed. "Compared to my current apartment, it's not too bad at all. My bedroom and living room are about this size together."

Without thinking, she reached out to put a hand on his wrist. "I really do want to thank you for putting your life on hold to help me, Andre."

He stiffened at her touch, but didn't pull away. "To be blunt, there wasn't much to put on hold. I've been drifting a bit since retiring, and it's good to feel needed again."

"I hope I don't need you too much...with the stalker I mean."

He smiled. "I hope you don't either, but I'm here."

She nodded and stepped back out of the room so he could make his way to his car to retrieve his things. As she watched him walk through her front door, ensuring it was locked behind him, she felt safer than she had in a long time. She wasn't certain if the possible stalking situation had been preying heavily on her mind and she'd refused to see it, or if there was simply something about Andre's presence.

The man himself radiated strength and confidence despite the slight stiffness when he moved, and his obvious stiffness that suggested he wasn't in top physical shape. Even with his injuries, she had no doubt he would protect her if it was necessary.

The only question was, who was going to protect her from Andre, and her raging attraction to the bodyguard?

AFTER TAKING MEDICAL retirement from the U.S. Marshals, Andre had simplified his life. He'd stripped down to the essentials and moved away from Las Vegas. He had a brother and a cousin in L.A., so it had seemed like a logical place to settle, and he had moved with only what would fit in the back of his Mini Cooper.

During the months he'd been in L.A., he'd kept his existence equally sparse, not collecting a lot of new things along the way. In some ways, L.A. felt like a weigh station, and he hadn't yet decided what he was on the way toward, but didn't want to be weighed down by unnecessary things.

That made it easy to pack up most of his stuff before meeting with his prospective new client, and he was able to bring everything that he had brought with him up in a single load. He didn't like leaving her alone in the apartment even for a few minutes, though he wasn't entirely certain if that was because his instincts were screaming that she was in danger, or because she was the first woman he'd found attractive since the shooting and subsequent recovery.

He shouldn't find her attractive at all if he wanted to keep her safe and protect her. Being drawn to her could cost him his edge, but he wasn't willing to walk away and leave her to someone else's protection. He'd made the offer, because he genuinely believed she would be better off with a team of security people, but he hadn't been too disappointed when she'd declined and once again insisted she just wanted him.

Lord knows he wanted her, and that was dangerous. With her perfectly creamy complexion, which contrasted starkly with her dark hair and dark eyes, she was a lethal combination. In that white, loosely draped lounge set she wore, he'd managed to catch tantalizing glimpses of the figure underneath, and it had taken recitation of every baseball score he could recall to stave off an erection when she'd accidentally revealed most of her shoulder and part of her arm.

How ridiculously juvenile to be reacting so strongly to commonplace body parts that he saw every day on millions of women in the city. Being L.A., he often saw far more than a shoulder, so it was enough to both embarrass and amuse him that he'd responded so powerfully to such a small view of her body.

He'd have to be on his guard, both to protect her against her stalker and to quell the attraction before it could get out of hand. He needed a clear head to keep his client safe, and right now, his body was thinking with the wrong head. He had a job to do, and he couldn't let his lustful thoughts distract him from it. Taking care of Dr. Soal was more important than taking her, and he'd just have to remind himself of that if he wavered.

Chapter Three

IT FELT STRANGE WALKING into the surgery center with Andre behind her. It'd been equally strange to share breakfast with him and try to make awkward small talk. It was akin to having a one-night stand that lasted through breakfast, without all of the sweaty fun parts that usually precede it.

Andre himself was clearly doing his best to put her at ease, and it wasn't because he made her nervous that things were awkward. He did make her nervous, but in a butterflies-in-the-stomach kind of way, not in a way that frightened her.

His presence was just a stark reminder of what she'd been trying to ignore and forget, which made her self-conscious. Each time she introduced him to someone in the center, she looped her arm through his and simply called him Andre, giving the impression they were in a relationship. All the while, she felt like there was a neon sign flashing "drama queen" across her forehead.

Misty was waiting for her in her office/dressing room, and she handed her the day's schedule on a tablet. Shannon looked at it, but had already reviewed it at home. Today, she chose fun scrubs with balloon animals all over them and a matching surgical cap. As she was placing the items on the shelf so she could change, she realized there was tension in the room and then blushed because she hadn't bothered to introduce Andre to Misty.

She walked over to stand by him, certain her body language was as awkward she felt. "Misty, this is Andre." She threaded her arm through his as she had done other times that morning, but it felt even stiffer and more unnatural than usual under Misty's watchful eyes. "Andre, this is my best friend, and the person who keeps me on track for everything, Misty."

Misty eyed Andre critically, examining him from head to toe, before looking at Shannon again. "Okay, what's going on?"

Shannon tried an awkward laugh. "What do you mean?"

"Who's the suit, and why is he here?"

It was kind of a funny question, since both of her work partners wore suits when they were on camera, but not conducting surgery. They also wore them all afternoon at the practice, though Shannon preferred a more business-casual look. "Andre and I have gotten closer."

Misty snorted. "Unless you got close in the last twelve hours, it didn't happen. I know you, and I know you aren't involved with anyone, so what's going on?"

Shannon let out a sigh, and her shoulders slumped. "I should have known I couldn't keep the truth from you. Andre is my bodyguard."

Misty let out a crow of satisfaction. "It's about time you took it seriously. So, what's the deal with the implied intimacy?"

Shannon realized she was still holding Andre's arm and let hers drop away slowly. She straightened her shoulders and took a step away, surprised at how bereft she felt at the distance between them. "I figured it would be less of a media circus if Andre pretends to be my boyfriend rather than my bodyguard."

Misty shook her head. "I know you're worried about seeming melodramatic about the whole thing, but you certainly wouldn't be the first celebrity who got stalked. It's nothing to be embarrassed about, Shannon."

She just shrugged. "I also wouldn't be the first celebrity to be accused of faking the whole thing for attention. Just because you know me well enough to know I wouldn't do that doesn't mean others wouldn't automatically jump to that assumption. I mean, my so-called stalker hasn't even done anything besides send some vague, weirdly disquieting notes to me."

Misty let out a sigh. "I know I can't change your mind about this, but I still think you're being silly trying to hide it. The more people who know about it, the safer you'll be."

Andre had been quiet until then, but now he cleared his throat. "That isn't necessarily true, Ms....?"

"Daniels," said Misty, crossing her arms over her chest. "And why is that?"

"The stalker has clearly fixated on Dr. Soal for some reason, but providing him with an audience might encourage things to escalate rather than neutralize the situation. If he knows the world's watching and waiting to see what he'll do, he might feel challenged to step up his game. It's better to be discreet about the situation."

After a moment, Misty's arms moved to her sides, and she nodded. "That makes sense. I'm glad she finally hired someone, Mr....?"

"Hart, but just call me Andre. If it's all right, I'll call you Misty. I assume it's well-known that you two are friends besides being coworkers, so it would seem strange if we aren't on a first-name basis as well."

Misty inclined her head, sending ripples of blonde waves cascading down her back. "Welcome to the team, Andre."

He held out his hand, and she shook it. Shannon was amused by the interplay between them, though slightly embarrassed when Misty squeezed his hand firmly before narrowing her eyes.

"Just make sure nothing happens to my friend."

"That's my job."

For some reason, Andre's stark words created a hollow feeling in her chest, and she had to clear her throat to dismiss the sensation. "Now that that's settled, why don't you both step out, so I can dress for surgery?" At her prodding, they both moved toward the door.

After changing, she stepped out of her dressing room a few minutes later to find Andre leaning against the wall, looking deceptively casual. She could tell immediately it was a front, simply by the way his shoulders were tense, and how close his hand was to the button of his jacket. She had watched him don it that morning, and the cut cleverly concealed the subtle bulge of his holster from prying eyes.

Watching him slip on the holster and put the gun in place after they'd eaten breakfast had been disquieting, since she'd never had a gun in her life, and had certainly never had one in her home. It also felt reassuring to know he was there, and he knew how to use it should the need arise.

Not that she expected her stalker to escalate to that point. She still felt somewhat ridiculous having hired Andre, but the peace of mind he gave her was worth dealing with the feeling that she had overreacted. It was better to be proactive than to do nothing, as Misty had said to her several times.

Andre fell into step beside her as she moved down the corridor. "I'll be in surgery most of the morning. There's an observation theater if you'd like to sit there, but you can't be in the OR."

Andre nodded. "I prefer to be at the door allowing direct entry, but I also need to know what's going on with you, so I'll probably split my time between the door and the observation room."

She nodded as they reached the scrub room, catching the attention of one of the interns passing by. "Rodney, could you please show Andre to the observation room for OR three?"

The eager young man nodded, and Andre gave her a long look before turning to walk away with the intern. Shannon wasn't certain what the look meant, but it was enough to send her heart rate accelerating and make her pulse flutter.

ANDRE OBSERVED THE surgery Shannon was currently conducting, suppressing a hint of queasiness at the sight. This was her third pediatric surgery of the morning, and he wasn't certain if it was the small size of the patient on the table, the way Shannon's scalpel slid through skin with no hesitation, or perhaps the huge TV mounted to the ceiling and angled downward that showed every detail of what she was doing that left him feeling queasy.

He had seen blood before. In fact, he'd been covered by his own blood a few months before after he'd been shot trying to protect his witness, Julia Dennings, from his crooked partner and a local mobster. It was different somehow to see it from this side, where it was simultaneously clinical and visceral.

Despite the uneasy state of his stomach, Andre appreciated and admired Shannon's obvious skill. Her hands never wavered, even on the smallest patient, and she seemed to know exactly what she was doing at all times. Watching her operate just gave him another reason to be impressed by her quiet strength and innate grace.

It certainly didn't rev up his libido, but the sight enhanced his attraction to her. Knowing it was dangerous to find her attractive didn't invalidate the emotion. It was a relief to look away from the screen and walk out of the observation room, taking the route that had started to become familiar as he made subtle security rounds, checking everything he could.

He stood outside the door to the OR for a short time, watching people come and go, but no one behaved with any hint of suspicion. Hardly any of them even looked at him or the OR. The looks he received were mostly of the female persuasion, and it made him grin. It was flattering to be found attractive, especially in Hollywood, where just about everyone was more beautiful than average. For those who weren't, they came to places like Shannon's practice to become so.

His grin faded slightly when he realized most of those flirtatious looks sent his way would fade if they saw the scars his suit hid. The scars might fade further in time, but they would never disappear. He was self-conscious about them, though he tried not to be, and it was part of the reason he'd avoided being intimate with a woman since he'd been shot.

Perhaps that was the only reason he was drawn to Dr. Soal. He was likely to be in her proximity for at least the next few weeks, and perhaps any woman would have awakened his suppressed sex drive if he was with her in close quarters often enough. In fact, he should arrange for Jared Silver to watch over the doctor for a few hours while he went out and found someone with whom to scratch the itch, which should allow him to think completely clearly again and set aside any feelings of attraction to his client.

As though his thoughts had summoned the man, his cell phone rang and "Silver" appeared on his screen. "Hello, Jared."

"Hey, Andre. I just wanted to check in with you and see if you've settled in?"

"I'm getting settled in, and everything's going okay at the moment."

Jared sounded relieved. "So she did hire you? I was afraid she'd be too stubborn when it came down to it."

"I think she sees the wisdom in having protection."

Jared gave an indulgent chuckle. "I knew I could wear her down eventually."

Andre didn't like his tone, but it took him a moment to realize why. It was too familiar and too intimate, as though the detective knew Shannon better than he should have as the investigator for her case. "How well do you know the doctor?"

"Well enough," he said in a slightly suggestive manner. "I'd like to know her better, but who wouldn't?"

"I don't need to remind you the importance of maintaining a professional distance, do I, Detective Silver?"

Jared chuckled, sounding completely at ease. "Relax there, Andre. I wouldn't let my personal relationship with the doctor interfere with my professional obligations to keep her safe. That's why you're there. If I felt insecure about the thought, there's no way I would have recommended you for the job. I would've stuck with one of the local firms who specialize in female bodyguards."

Andre wasn't certain, but he thought his old friend was suddenly warning him away from getting involved with Shannon beyond a professional capacity. He was fairly confident it wasn't because Jared was afraid Andre couldn't maintain the focus he needed to keep her safe. It was all about the other man subtly marking his territory. The question was, did Shannon know Jared was claiming her as his?

"Do you need anything, buddy? If you need to go out for a few hours, or if you're getting stir crazy, give me a call, and I'll come stay with Shannon."

Though he'd just had the thought that he should do that very thing, Andre grimaced at the idea. "No, everything's fine. I just got here, so I don't need any downtime yet. Thanks for the offer though." He made a point to interject genuine-sounding gratitude into his voice, because he certainly wasn't feeling it.

He'd just disconnected from the detective when the first of the camera crew exited the OR. They would have stopped by to scrub out, if he had his terminology correct, and now they were bustling down the hallway, not sparing him a look at all. That was perfect, and the reaction he wanted. He wanted to blend into the backgrounds, and appear not only nonthreatening, but practically nonexistent. His job was to be a shadow for Shannon, and it would be better if she didn't see him either. Unfortunately, with her unorthodox insistence that they pose as a couple, that wasn't practical or possible.

When she emerged from the operating room several minutes later, removing her cap to allow her dark hair to fall around her pale face, a skip of excitement in his chest betrayed his reaction, at least to himself. Her situation was dangerous, and the relationship they were pretending to have was unusual, but he was grateful she wasn't looking through him when she flashed him a brilliant smile. It made her already beautiful face light up and stoked the flames of the desire he felt for her. He couldn't hold back his own wide grin, though he feared he was smiling so widely, he looked like the village idiot.

She didn't speak as she walked in step beside him, but their shoulders brushed, and she didn't pull away. Even when they reached her dressing room/office, and he escorted her inside to ensure it was clear, she didn't move very far from him. The need for pretense was over by that point, but she seemed to have forgotten that it was all pretend. Andre was quickly forgetting that himself, and though that should've alarmed him, it didn't. Instead, it just felt right.

Chapter Four

THE PAST THREE DAYS had been quiet, and Shannon was starting to think she had definitely overreacted by hiring a bodyguard. She hadn't heard from her stalker since Andre had entered the picture, so she was speculating maybe he had scared the stalker away, even without making it known he was her bodyguard. Perhaps the person had grown bored of tormenting her and had moved on. She hadn't relaxed her guard just yet, but she was hopeful that the whole thing was over, and Andre had been the solution.

She was also disappointed by the idea, because it meant she might soon need to dismiss Andre. If there was no stalker, there was no reason to keep him around, and though she'd only known him three days, the idea of not seeing him again caused a hitch in her chest.

They were relaxing on her balcony, having just finished the shrimp scampi Andre had made from scratch, as they each enjoyed a glass of white wine. She was feeling mellow, and her guard was definitely down. Her gaze kept drifting to Andre's mouth, and she wondered what his lips would taste like.

Her busy schedule rarely allowed time for romantic pursuits, and the few men she had tried dating over the last couple of years had either been too busy in their own right to make something work, the chemistry had been lacking, or they had simply sought her out because she was a moderate celebrity. It was different with Andre, and she was less tense around him. Maybe it was the second glass of wine, or perhaps it was just his soothing presence combined with the lack of activity from her stalker, but she wasn't on edge at the moment, leaving her open to anything.

It was a dangerous state to be in with a man she was attracted to, one who was probably not interested in her. She couldn't say definitively whether he was or wasn't. Andre had certainly never made an inappropriate move, and he maintained an aloof distance between them when it was just the two of them with no need to have the pretense of a relationship.

But his eyes sometimes looked at her with what she swore was longing, so she was uncertain how he truly felt. Three days into their pseudo-relationship, she certainly couldn't imagine asking him where their relationship was headed—especially since they didn't really have a relationship beyond employer and employee.

That wasn't strictly true though, was it? Of course she had friends among her employees, Misty being chief among them, but she wasn't in the habit of sharing intimate meals on the balcony with them, no matter how good of a friend they were. She could argue that he was in her home as her guest, so of course she would share a meal with him, but they had lingered over dinner and conversation for at least ninety minutes, and now they were still sitting in pleasant silence as they drank their wine.

She couldn't speak for him, but she felt no need to fill the quiet with conversation. The moment was just soothing, and she was completely relaxed—except for her nerve endings, which were attuned to every subtle move Andre made. It was only when he shifted in his chair, actually putting him a few inches away from her, that she realized she wasn't as relaxed as she had pretended. Part of her was on edge, hoping he would make a move, and that move would be toward her rather than away. She let out a long sigh and put down her glass.

He set aside his wine, his sole glass of the evening, and looked at her. "What's on your mind?"

Shannon shrugged. "I was just thinking that your presence seems to have quelled the stalker. We probably don't need to do this any longer." Was she really suggesting that, or was she fishing for him to tell her he didn't want to leave? She couldn't answer that question, which made her feel flustered and silly, like a teenager with a crush.

He frowned. "You shouldn't just assume that. Have there been other times when your stalker has gone quiet?"

Shannon licked her lips, thinking back. "I guess he didn't correspond every single day. But he hasn't gone three days without anything since I first noticed he was corresponding regularly."

Andre nodded. "It could be that he's given up, but it could be that he's also gearing up for the next stage. Stalkers usually escalate. Sometimes, it's a slow progression, and sometimes they rev up to full-on crazy without any real notice. Unless you tell me to, I'm not going anywhere just yet."

She smiled at him. "I don't want you to go anywhere, Andre."

He grinned. "Then I'm here and all yours for as long as you want me."

She had the craziest urge to say forever, but managed to stifle the impulse. "Thank you, Andre." She reached out to put her hand over his, squeezing lightly. "I know you're being paid to act as my support, but I certainly appreciate having you here."

His expression was brooding for a moment, and his hand turned in hers, his palm and fingers encasing her hand. "Some things are more important than money. I'm not here because you're paying me to be. I want to be here with you, Shannon."

They fell into that comfortable silence again, and her gaze locked with his. Their eyes were saying things that their mouths dared not share yet. She marveled that the simple way they were holding hands and their nonverbal communication could make her feel closer to him than she had felt to previous partners after sharing her body.

HER STALKER BROKE HIS silence the next morning, and unlike what she'd shared with Andre, it hadn't been a comfortable silence. She arrived in her dressing room with Andre in tow to find Misty waiting. Her friend's anxious expression told her there was something waiting from the stalker. She was unsurprised when Misty handed her a padded envelope, and she pulled out the paper, which was thicker than usual.

Andre intercepted it, taking it from her fingers. The more he read, the darker his expression became. He let out a snarling sound and looked like he wanted to throw it across the room for a moment before taking a deep breath.

"What does it say?" asked Shannon.

"He's definitely watching you. He knows I'm your bodyguard and not your boyfriend."

"How do you know?"

Andre hesitated for a moment, looking like he wanted to withhold the paper. Instead, he angled so she could see it. "Don't touch it any more than you already have, because I want to get it dusted for fingerprints."

"Sure." She leaned closer, spending a moment inhaling his scent, before her gaze moved from the arm of his suit jacket against her cheek to look over his shoulder at the paper he held.

Her stomach dropped as she read it. Her stalker had clearly decided to do away with subtlety. He ranted how she had betrayed him, and that she was foolish if she thought Andre Hart, a disgraced U.S. Marshal, could keep her safe. One line in particular caught her attention. *Ask him about Lisa Wentworth, and see if you're still safe.*

She looked up, finding Andre's gaze waiting to meet hers. "Who is Lisa Wentworth?"

"She was a witness under my care earlier in my career. I was a new Marshal, and I didn't keep her safe enough. She was killed by the cartel against whom she was due to testify. I failed her, but I won't fail you. Losing Lisa made me more determined than ever to take care of anyone else under my care, and I've done that. You have nothing to fear about my competence, but if you'd prefer a different guard, I understand."

Misty gasped. "Maybe you should, Shannon. Someone else. Someone who isn't a disgraced U.S. Marshal."

Shannon glared at her friend. "Andre isn't disgraced. He was medically retired due to a disability after being shot protecting a witness. There's no one I trust more with my safety than Andre, and the stalker's not going to undermine my confidence in him."

Misty looked hurt for a moment, but then blinked, and her expression cleared. "If that's what you want, and you feel comfortable with him, then you know what you're doing."

Shannon squared her shoulders. "I do know what I'm doing, but thank you." She allowed her tone to soften slightly, making a conscious effort to release her irritation at Misty questioning Andre's competence. It was a natural reaction, and she knew her friend was just looking out for her, but she was protective of Andre. That wasn't how the relationship was supposed to work, but it didn't lessen her need to defend him.

"Do you still feel like operating this morning, or are you rattled?" Misty was back to all business.

"I'll operate. It'll take more than this rubbish to keep me from my patients."

SHE EMERGED FROM THE clinic that evening with Andre at her side, and at first everything was as usual. Then suddenly, there was a crowd surrounding them. Cameras flashed, and reporters were screaming questions at her. She was dumbfounded and stopped, unable to move for a moment as she stared around and tried to comprehend what was happening. Finally, a few of the questions filtered through the other shouting the tried to drown them out.

"How long have you had a stalker?"

"Has he attacked you?"

"Is it true the man behind you is your bodyguard and not your boyfriend?"

She blinked at the questions almost as much as she blinked at the continuous flash of the cameras. Andre was there, wrapping his arm around her and pressing her close to his body as he shielded her while practically shoving his way through the crowd like a battering ram.

He didn't try to go for the parking garage, where her car was. Instead, he directed her toward a cab, and they squeezed in together. All the while, the reporters pressed around her, and even when they were in the car, they were tapping on the window and still shouting at her. It was her first real taste of the ugly side of the media.

"Just drive," barked Andre at the driver, who peeled away with a squeal of rubber.

Once they were underway, she could finally relax slightly. "How did they know?" she asked as she leaned back in the seat, her head resting on Andre's shoulder.

"Either someone leaked it, or your stalker himself let the word out. I think he's gearing up to escalate. You should withdraw from public life for a while. I have a cabin in Big Bear, and we could go there."

Shannon shook her head. "I'm not going to run away or let this guy intimidate me away from my life."

Andre sighed. "I can keep you safer when you're out of the public eye."

She shrugged a shoulder. "I'm not going to let him dictate to me how to live my life. I won't let you do that either, Andre, even if you're doing what you think is best."

He ran a hand through his stubbly curls before letting out a frustrated sigh. "Fine, but if he escalates further, I want you to promise you'll at least consider the idea."

She snuggled against him, knowing she was crossing a line she shouldn't as she allowed his arm to enfold her, and her head to rest on his chest. "I promise to think about it if the need arises, but I know you'll keep me safe."

"This is a bad idea."

She lifted her head from his chest, which brought her lips temptingly close to his. "It's a bad idea to continue living my life?"

He shook his head. "It's a bad idea to be this close to you. I should push you away."

Shannon licked her lips, her gaze on his as she did so. "I should let you push me away."

She held her breath as she waited to see if he would, but his tension gradually relaxed, and he didn't push her away. He didn't pull her closer either, but she was still lying against him, her head on his chest when she lowered it again as she realized he wouldn't be receptive to the kiss that she so badly wanted to give him.

She was certain he would physically want it, but he was clearly conflicted between duty and desire, and she didn't want to push Andre to do something he was opposed to, no matter how badly she wanted to feel his lips against hers. Instead, she settled for the safety of his arms, and that was certainly something to savor as well.

His heart thumped steadily against her ear as the driver took them toward her condo, and she felt safe and relaxed despite the incident with the media, and the note from her stalker that morning. Andre's presence was reassuring, and even if they never moved beyond that, and it was all she had with him, she was happy to have it for that moment.

Chapter Five

SHANNON HAD CALMED considerably by the next morning, especially when there had been no sign of paparazzi near her condo. When she'd left Andre's arms after departing the cab, he hadn't offered her the comfort of them again, but that was for the best. She was emotionally vulnerable yesterday, but this morning was a new day, and she wasn't going to surrender to the urge pushing her toward Andre—especially since he was far too professional to allow it anyway.

Andre was right behind her when she entered her dressing room that morning, and she scanned for signs of something else from her stalker, but found everything in order. With a slight bounce in her step, she moved to the scrubs and selected Rudy's favorite pair, the ones with pink and purple elephants all over the top and matching pink pants.

Andre stepped closer to her. "You seem cheerful this morning in light of everything that happened. Are you all right?"

She nodded as she looked at him peripherally, not allowing herself to stare into the tempting warmth of his brown eyes. "I haven't lost my mind or forgotten the seriousness of the situation, Andre. Today's just a good day. I'll be operating on my favorite patient this morning, and then I'll spend some time with him this afternoon. It's my only obligation today."

"Who is this favorite patient of yours?

Was she imagining he sounded faintly jealous? It was probably wishful thinking, but she hoped it was true. Not wanting to allow herself to be vulnerable was a completely different thing from wishing to have him open up to her. Even if it was reckless and stupid under the circumstances, she wanted to get closer to her pretend boyfriend.

"Rudy's been my patient since he was three. He's nine now, and he's on a rough road. This is his fifteenth surgery."

Andre grimaced. "Poor kid. What's wrong with him?"

"He has Hemifacial Microsomia or HFM. Half of his face is underdeveloped, and he has a severe case of it. It can be a mild problem, but it was fairly extensive in Rudy. We've spent the last six years rebuilding that side of his face one slow step at a time."

"That sounds tough. It must be hard on his parents as well."

Shannon snorted before she could stop herself. "Don't get me started on those people. Rudy was born in India, where his mother abandoned him at an orphanage. Considering the medical and economic conditions there, I can certainly understand her actions. I'd like to think she was doing the best she could and hoping they could get care for her son when she couldn't."

He arched a brow. "So how did he end up here in the U.S.? Does he travel from India for care?"

Shannon tucked her hair into a cap before answering. "He was adopted from the orphanage when he was two. His adoptive parents were aware he had HFM, but they didn't know just how bad it was until he got to the States. They spent about six months playing parent through the ordeals before deciding it was too much for them. They relinquished their rights to custody, and he became a ward of the state. I've made it my business to stay involved in Rudy's life to ensure he gets the surgeries he needs, and I keep hoping someone will adopt him."

"Someone willing to give him a permanent home," said Andre, his tone thick with disgust. "I look forward to meeting this special young man."

"You can this afternoon. Today, we're rebuilding the bone around his eye." A hint of anxiety shot through her. She didn't doubt her skill in completing the surgery, but it was always harder to operate on Rudy than her other patients. In her heart, she knew she was too emotionally involved with the little boy, but it hadn't made her sloppy or careless as a doctor. Nor had it made it impossible to do the difficult things thus far, so she had no intention of relinquishing his care to someone else unless or until she discovered she couldn't be impartial enough to continue providing his care in the future.

Andre walked her out of the dressing room, and she parted from him at the OR. When she stepped up to the scrub sink, all of her anxiety fell away. In this area, she could be at peace and focus on what had to be done without worrying about her stalker, or how she would handle the burgeoning relationship with Andre. Right now, she was simply Dr. Soal, and it was all about the job at hand.

THE SURGERY WAS A SUCCESS, as she'd expected, and Shannon sat with him in the recovery room. When he started to stir, she slipped away to change out of the scrubs and into something more comfortable for the afternoon. He wouldn't convalesce at the surgery center, due to his age and possible complications. Instead, he would be transferred to the hospital across the street in the pediatric ward, and she wanted to be in his room waiting for him when he arrived.

She frowned when she saw Andre waiting in the hallway. "What's wrong?"

He laughed, but it was an awkward sound. "I watched more of the surgery today. I've seen all kinds of things, but I guess I don't have the stomach for that—especially knowing how much you care about the little boy you were operating on. I don't know how you do it."

She shrugged. "It never occurred to me to want to be a doctor, at least not until I was seventeen. I had a serious car accident, and the plastic surgeons not only restored my face, they made me *practically flawless*." She touched her face self-consciously with her freshly scrubbed hands as she remembered how she used to look compared to how she did now.

"It was unsettling to suddenly be an object of attention, and though I wasn't entirely happy with the changes for a long time, I still appreciated all their skills. It fascinated me how much they could transform my features, both from the Plain Jane I had been, and the destroyed bone structure from trauma. Somehow, I just naturally gravitated toward the career from that point."

"That makes a lot of sense."

She paused to arch a brow at him when he stopped walking. "What do you mean?"

"For one thing, it explains your reticence to believe you're being stalked or in serious danger. And it also tells me why you want to fly under the radar. You spent years shying away and not being in the spotlight, and now that you are, you still haven't quite found your groove."

His words stung, though she couldn't explain entirely why. Shannon forced an uncomfortable laugh. "I didn't know you were also a psychologist along with a bodyguard."

"You don't have to admit it, but it makes sense to me." He shrugged. "How about you introduce me to Rudy now?"

She was certain pleasure suffused her expression, because warmth flowed through her. "Gladly."

It was nerve-racking to step outside of the surgical center a few moments later, and she scanned the area for any sign of reporters, but they had surprisingly backed off.

When she voiced that thought aloud, Andre shook his head. "They haven't really backed off. They're simply being held in check right now by Detective Silver, along with a few other people backing the production company that produces your show. They could still spring on you at any time, so don't wander from my sight."

She brushed her hand against his, not entirely certain if it was accidentally or on purpose. "I have no intention of moving from your side, Andre."

His hand twined with hers, and their fingers grasped each other as they walked. Neither of them spoke, and she was careful not to look down or even really think about the fact that they were holding hands. Shannon wasn't certain if it was to maintain the pretense of their relationship, or if it was for real. It felt real to her.

They reached the hospital a couple of minutes later, and they were in Rudy's room a few seconds before the nurse pushing the bed entered, bearing her tiny favorite patient. He looked about the size of a six-year-old, which was partly genetics, and partly poor nutrition the first couple of years of his life.

His face lit up when he saw her, just as it had that morning when she spoke to him for a few minutes in the OR, before his anesthesia took effect. He'd been excited to see the elephants and was fascinated with them. He claimed to remember one living in his village in India, but Shannon doubted he would have been old enough to retain the impression.

"How are you feeling?" That came out in her doctor tone. As she asked, she moved around to examine him, looking at his vitals as they hooked up the proper machines.

"My face hurts." He lifted his hand for a moment before letting it fall back on the white sheet, clearly still not strong enough to complete the maneuver. That was to be expected from lingering effects of anesthesia, and it was better that he didn't handle the area anyway. "Did you give me a third eye, Doc?"

She laughed, recalling his request to have a third eye inserted in the middle of his forehead at their last pre-op appointment. "I'm sorry, but I couldn't secure a fake eye for you. They all just looked cheesy."

Her little patient feigned disappointment. "I was looking forward to having an extra eye. It would really give people something to laugh at."

His words sent a pang through her chest, but she managed to maintain a smile. "There's no reason for people to laugh."

Rudy tilted his head slightly, giving her a look full of disbelief. "I know you love me, Doc Shannon, but that ain't true."

"Isn't true," she corrected automatically. "And it is true. You looked different, but there's nothing to laugh at."

Rudy snorted. "Try telling that to the kids at school." He sounded brave, but his veneer was paper-thin, and he appeared to be on the edge of tears.

In an effort to lighten the moment, Shannon pointed at Andre, who stepped forward. "This is my friend, Andre, and you don't see him laughing."

Andre held out his hand, letting it hang there for a moment before it dropped to his side when the boy eyed him doubtfully, but didn't take it. "I don't see anything to laugh at, Rudy."

Rudy rolled his eyes, though the one was heavily bandaged. "Sure you don't. You two are perfect, so you couldn't understand."

"I'm not perfect." As he spoke, Andre shrugged off his jacket, and Shannon's eyes widened at the sight of his gun. Of course she'd seen it before, but it was easy to forget when it was hidden under the coat. He had his body angled so that Rudy couldn't see it, and she watched with curiosity as he started unbuttoning his shirt.

"What's he doing?" Rudy asked her.

Shannon shook her head. "I'm not sure."

"If this is how you say hello, you're a weird one."

She laughed at Rudy's comment, and Andre chuckled too. He didn't unbutton his shirt all the way—just a few buttons at the bottom so he could lift it up to show his abdomen.

A series of fresh scars marred his skin; some still pink, and other parts starting to fade to white. She grimaced at the sight, but not because it was ugly. It was just a reminder of how close he'd come to death, and what had cost him his career with the marshals.

Rudy moved a little bit, looking like he was trying to get closer. "That's wicked." He seemed more intrigued and more interested in Andre now. "How'd you do it?"

"I was shot trying to protect a witness. I used to be a U.S. Marshal." Andre's lean fingers fastened his buttons again and casually tucked the shirt into his pants. When he shrugged on his jacket half a minute later, the gun was once again firmly out of sight.

"That was your idea of protecting her?" Rudy sounded skeptical.

Shannon winced, knowing it was a sensitive subject for him and automatically assuming he was talking about Lisa Wentworth. It only occurred to her as he spoke again that the scars were too fresh to be from Lisa Wentworth's case.

"It was the best I could do, and Julia is just fine these days. She lives on a ranch in Montana with her husband, Justin. He and I were in the military together, and he took care of her after I was shot. She took care of herself too, and she's happy as can be. They're expecting a baby in...seven months, I think?"

That seemed to satisfy Rudy's curiosity, and it was obvious the day's events were starting to catch up with him. His uncovered eyelid was blinking almost continuously, and he was slumping against the pillow. "How do you think it will look when it heals, Doc Shannon?"

She moved closer to hold his hand briefly. "I think it's going to look like a million bucks."

Rudy grinned. "That's probably what it cost too."

She leaned closer, lowering her voice in a conspiratorial fashion. "Not for you. You get the friend discount, so it's only half a million."

"Just send me the bill." His eyes drifted shut with the last words, and he was soon snoring.

"He fell asleep quickly," said Andre as he came to stand beside her.

She reluctantly let go of the boy's hand. "It happens that way sometimes with anesthesia. You can be alert one moment and out the next. He could be like this for the next twenty-four hours or so."

Andre took the hand she relinquished from Rudy, wrapping it in his fingers. It was just the two of them in there, aside from her sleeping patient. "You really love the kid, don't you?"

Shannon nodded and blinked at the unexpected prick of moisture in her eyes. "His life has been unfair, but he's still funny and bright. I admire his strength and ability to keep going."

"He is a charmer."

They shared a silence for a moment that seemed to stretch. Finally, they exited the room by mutual unspoken agreement, their hands still entwined.

Chapter Six

"REMEMBER TO STAY CLOSE to me," said Andre. Shannon seemed to be distracted, so he took her hand and squeezed lightly to get her attention before he opened the door. "Remember, stay with me."

She nodded, and her fingers clutched his. "Don't worry. I have no intention of straying from your side. I don't really like these things, and they're even worse because I see all the reporters out there waiting for us."

He wanted her in the right frame of mind, so he squeezed her hand yet again. "They're here to film all the celebrities that came to contribute to your foundation, so don't let them rattle you. They're still speculating about us, but they won't be swamping you tonight. The security around this place is tight. I made sure of that before we ever left your house."

She smiled, and the curve of her full lips, painted a bright berry-purple, was almost enough temptation to make him lower his head and see if they tasted as luscious as they looked. He forced back the thought, crushing it ruthlessly with the reminder that her safety was in his hands, and he couldn't get careless or allow the attraction he felt to overwhelm him.

"I'm ready," she said with a hint of false bravado.

He didn't think she truly was, but he was also certain she wouldn't be any readier than she was at that moment. He opened the door and slid out first, looking around carefully before extending his hand to help her out. Even in the moment, when he was hyperaware of security, he still spent a half-second casting an appreciative glance at her. He'd seen her in the finery at her condo, but it was difficult not to stare at her in the berry-purple dress that hugged her curves before flaring out to swish at her feet in a fall of sequins and tulle.

She wore insanely high heels that brought her height almost to his, and they were most definitely fuck-me pumps. It was all he could think about every time he glanced at her feet, so he studiously avoided doing so as he took her arm and led her inside the hotel as quickly as possible. "Where are we going?"

"The Children's Gala." She waved to a sign nearby that directed them toward the correct ballroom. "It's not just my charity, you know? It's a conglomerate of charities that team up for this event every year and then split the proceeds."

"Can a donor make a donation directly to the charity of their choice?"

"Of course they can."

"In that case, I have something for you." Andre reached into his jacket and found the check in his pocket before handing it to her. "It isn't much, but seeing what you do for Rudy and the other kids inspires me."

She frowned before looking at him. "This is basically the amount of money I'm paying you to be my bodyguard."

He shrugged. "That's a job for which I will happily volunteer."

For a moment, she looked like she wanted to argue, and then her dark eyes looked moist as she started to blink. Shannon cleared her throat and made a production of putting the check in her evening bag. "Thank you."

The words were simple, but heartfelt, and he wasn't looking for a string of endless gratitude. He'd done what felt right, and he appreciated her ability to move past it quickly. It left him feeling unaccountably raw in the moment.

The Gala was a surprise, featuring entertainment acts and even a charity auction, along with a sumptuous dinner. Andre was afraid he might have to undo the top button of his pants as he leaned back in his chair at the end of the meal. "That was amazing. I see why people pay a thousand dollars a plate."

"Do you want to hear a secret?" At his nod, she leaned closer to pitch her voice lower. "The caterer donates her time and provides all the food at cost. Her little brother survived a brain tumor, so it's her way of giving back."

"Don't let word get out, or people might complain about the thousand-dollar price tag." They were definitely moving in a different crowd than he was accustomed to. The people circulating in the room could absolutely afford the price they paid for their plate and ticket, along with dropping substantial donations. He'd seen three Oscar winners, an Academy Award winner, and four Grammy nominees in the last hour. They all seemed determined to out-donate each other, which could only benefit the charities involved.

"I have to visit the ladies' room."

Andre pushed back from the table as she started to rise, glad when she didn't protest the escort. He would've insisted on accompanying her no matter what, though he allowed her to slip inside by herself. It made him antsy that he wasn't able to check the bathroom beforehand, but he had to let her enter anyway. It would have been awkward and raised questions he was certain she didn't want to deal with if he'd insisted on searching the restroom before allowing her to enter.

Andre glanced at his watch and leaned against the wall, waiting for Shannon to finish. He'd been there about a minute when a man with a famous face stepped out of the men's room wearing a velvet tuxedo. He nodded at Andre and smiled. "Seems like we spend half our lives waiting on our women, doesn't it?"

Andre nodded his response, but was glad when the man moved on without trying to further the conversation. He didn't want to lose track of the time. Already, Shannon had been in there a couple of minutes, which seemed excessive to him, but he knew women did all kinds of weird things in the bathroom, like fix their hair and put on new lipstick.

He was prepared to give her thirty seconds more before he tapped on the door when he heard a bang. He didn't have to think about acting. His feet were already running, and his shoulder slammed into the door as he reached for the pistol in his holster.

He hoped he was overreacting, but he wasn't surprised to find Shannon scuffling with someone. The person looked big and bulky and wore a nondescript black sweat suit. He was trying to subdue Shannon, and there was a cleaning cart with a conveniently empty laundry bag waiting nearby. That would have been how he planned to transport Shannon from the restroom.

"Release her." He removed the safety on his gun, which made an ominous click that he hoped carried to the stalker.

The man froze, clearly weighing his options. Half a second later, he virtually flung Shannon in Andre's direction. Andre wanted to chase the stalker, but he couldn't let Shannon fall or get injured. He caught her, and they both slammed backward into the wall from the force of the collision. In the process, the stalker ran past them, moving far faster than his bulky frame would have suggested he could.

Shannon laid against him for a minute, her body trembling. "He was waiting when I came out of the stall. It's a good thing I got to pee first, or this dress might've been ruined." She gave a shaky laugh that quickly dissolved into a sob, and he held her in his arms. He needed to call Jared, along with coordinate with the hotel security to try to find the stalker, but she needed him more at the moment.

"You can't make these kinds of public appearances anymore until we've tracked down the stalker."

She lifted her head, and her lips wobbled for a moment before her expression firmed. "It's like letting him dictate my life."

Andre nodded. "It is, but at least you're still alive. He's obviously escalating, and he intended to kidnap you tonight. You can't give him another opportunity, so you need to bow out of the spotlight for a while."

She let out a sigh. "Would do you suggest I do?"

"I think it's time to go to my cabin in Big Bear. Will you do that for me?" He was certain it cost her a great deal of pride to relent with a nod a moment later. "I know it's not what you want to do, but my first priority is keeping you safe."

"I know, but I resent it like hell that I'm the one who has to put my life on hold because some freak is obsessed with me. It isn't fair."

He cupped her face in his hands. "No, it isn't, but I promise you I'll stop him as soon as I can."

Her obvious faith in him shone in her eyes, and it left him choked up for a moment. "I know you will. Just don't get yourself killed trying to save me."

"That's part of the job."

Somehow, she managed a small smile. "If you promise not to get yourself killed, maybe we can arrange a bonus."

Andre gave her a crooked half-grin as his thoughts suddenly provided him with myriad bonus options he'd like to explore. "Afraid I can't promise that, but I can promise I'll guard your body with my life."

"Just my body and not my mind?" She seemed to be using humor to hide how close she was to falling apart.

"You, Dr. Soal, are the total package." He let his hands drop away from her face and put one around her waist. "Let's deal with this and get on the road as soon as possible. I want you out of this town and safer."

"You just want to have me all to yourself." She said the words in a teasing fashion.

Andre didn't reply, not wanting to confirm just how accurate they were. He shouldn't want that, but he craved it with every fiber of his being. Taking her away from L.A. was about keeping her safe, but he wasn't certain how he was going to keep himself safe from the temptation his client represented. Being alone with her would be like playing with fire, but he was certain it was the best course of action to get her out of the stalker's range. He would just have to exercise all of his willpower to ensure that getting her away from the stalker didn't end up putting her in his bed.

Chapter Seven

THEY HAD BARELY ARRIVED back at the condo before the doorbell rang. Andre sent Shannon on down the hall. "Go pack what you'll need for a few days. There's a washer and dryer at the cabin if we're there longer than we expect."

She looked uncertainly at her door. "But...?"

He shook his head. "I'll deal with it." He had a feeling who it would be standing on the other side, and he wasn't surprised to see Detective Silver when he opened the door a moment later. Their conversation had been terse when he'd called to apprise him of the situation.

Silver didn't even wait until the door had closed behind him before he started in. "You can't just take her away to the middle of nowhere. It's not fair to her, and it's the very thing she doesn't want."

Andre shrugged. "It might not be what she wants, but Shannon recognizes the necessity for now. I think it became real to her tonight. It was still sort of abstract until the stalker laid his hands on her."

"It's been real all along, and taking her away to guard her by yourself is foolhardy. You should take several people with you. I have some time coming up that I could take. I could trade with—"

"That won't be necessary. I have it covered, and if I need backup, I have people I can call."

Jared glared at him. "Suddenly I'm not a person you can call?"

Andre didn't comment either way. "I understand this is frustrating for you, since it's your investigation, but this is what Shannon wants to do."

"I believe I'll ask her myself."

As he moved past him, Andre reached out to take his arm. "You won't be letting yourself into her bedroom. If you want to ask her, you'll

">

wait right here, because that's a line you aren't going to cross." Partially, it was determination to keep Silver in line, but it was also an edict issued because of his discomfort at allowing Silver to be alone with Shannon. It wasn't jealousy, or at least not *just* jealousy. He was starting to wonder about the good detective, who might not be so good after all.

"Get your hand off me, Hart. Shannon won't mind if I pop into her room."

"When did you become on a first-name basis with her?"

With a melodramatic shrug that dislodged his hand, Silver glared at him. "We're very good friends, and you're standing in the way of that. I don't believe you've given Shannon a list of all of her possible options, and I intend to see that she gets each one before she picks."

Andre arched a brow and crossed his arms over his chest, temporarily allowing his posture to relax slightly when Jared made no further move to walk down the hallway. "What are these options you have in mind?"

He just glared at him. "You can hear when I lay it out for Shannon."

"Lay what out for me?" asked the doctor as she appeared the hallway with what looked like a carry-on bag in her hands. Andre had expected her to bring more since they were going to be away for a few days, and he was pleasantly surprised that she'd kept it efficient.

"I don't know what Hart told you, but running away to hide alone with him in some cabin up north isn't the best course of action."

Shannon frowned. "What would you suggest, Detective Silver?"

Andre barely hid a grin when she used the detective's last name, making Jared grimace.

"We can get you round-the-clock protection here."

"No, you can't," she responded, confused. "He hasn't escalated to the point of violence."

Andre reminded Shannon gently, "Tonight, he could've been very violent. It's possible with Angus Calvin's connections, and your limited fame—but unlikely–the detective could get round-the-clock security for you now, which would probably entail a patrol car sitting outside your door twenty-four hours a day, which might be sufficient when combined with my presence."

She frowned. "It doesn't sound very safe, since the stalker will know where to find me. What other options do I have?"

"You could hire a cadre of bodyguards and not rely on just one." Silver glared in his direction. "Hart's giving you bad advice."

"What's the worst part?" Andre asked. "Is it the fact that I won't tell you where I'm taking her, or that we'll be there alone without you?"

His glare deepened, and Shannon seemed not to have heard Andre's quietly whispered comment.

"I have some vacation time, so I could take it while you stay with me, or I could come with the two of you."

Shannon stiffened slightly, but she wore a gracious smile when she shook her head. "That's a kind offer, Detective Silver, but I'm safe with Andre, and I trust him."

"But you don't trust me?" There was a hint of petulance in the question. "I've known you a long time, Dr. Soal. I wish you'd take that into consideration when making your decision. I just want what's best for you."

She smiled again, but moved away from him as she walked closer to Andre. He was pleased to see her natural caution. His senses were tingling, and he grew more suspicious of Silver by the moment. "I want the same thing for Shannon. I'll guard her with my life, and you'll be here trying to track down her stalker so she can come back home. That's where you're needed most, Detective Silver."

Jared looked like he wanted to argue for another moment, and then he sighed as he ran a hand through his dark hair. "Yeah, okay. Your point's taken, Hart. Dr. Soal, call me if you need anything."

"I'm afraid she won't be able to. She's leaving behind all of her electronic devices in case they're being monitored or tracked in some fashion."

"No, I'm not," said Shannon, sounding outraged.

"How are we supposed to stay in contact then, Mr. Hart?"

He took a card from his pocket and handed it to the other man. "This is my private cell, and there's no reason to leave it behind. It's a special edition that's been scrupulously combed by someone in the NSA, and no one's tracking it." His friend Olivia Irons had given him the technology on the sly, which was normally reserved for NSA agents and high-ranking government officials.

Silver tucked the card in his pocket with a resigned sigh. "Since I can't change your mind, I'll just wish you luck, Dr. Soal. I'll be in touch with you, Hart, and I expect you to look after our girl."

"Shannon's a strong, capable woman, but I'll do my best to keep her safe." There was a twinge in his stomach as he said the words, the phantom pain of the reminder of being shot trying to protect Julia Dennings. She was Julia Harbor now, he reminded myself, and living happily with Justin. Andre had saved her, even though he hadn't been able to save Lisa. Shannon was going to be another success story, and not a face that haunted him when he closed his eyes at night.

THEY WERE IN THE CAR, having covered about forty miles of the almost one-hundred-and-twenty-mile drive, when something Silver said surfaced in Andre's mind. "How long have you known Detective Silver?"

Shannon shrugged a slim shoulder, looking away from the mountain scenery the Jeep's headlights illuminated. "I don't really know him at all, other than through the investigation. About a year ago, I operated on his ex-girlfriend. She wanted a new set of boobs, and he came along to her pre-op appointment. He was there during the surgery and for her aftercare. I can give him credit for that, but I heard they didn't last much longer than that. At her six-month follow-up, they'd broken up."

"And then Detective Silver just happened to get your stalker case? That's an interesting coincidence."

Shannon shrugged, seeming oblivious to the dots Andre was connecting. "Yeah, I suppose it was."

He made a noncommittal sound and allowed silence to fill the car again. It was comfortable, and he was glad Shannon didn't feel the need to fill it with mindless chatter. It suited him, being on the quiet side, and her presence was naturally soothing.

And arousing as hell. That was an uncomfortable fact of life to which he still hadn't grown immune while being around her. More often than not, he was sporting an erection in her vicinity, and that was unlikely to change now that they were going to be in close proximity with each other. In fact, it would probably become a constant hard-on that he would have to hide behind everything. It was like having a flashback to his teenage years, and he didn't know whether to chuckle or moan in despair.

"How much farther is it?"

"Another hour or so. You look tired, Shannon."

Her sooty lashes rested against her pale cheeks for a moment before flickering upward. "I'm fine. Just a little tired, since it was such an eventful night, but I'd rather stay awake and make sure you don't fall asleep on the drive."

He looked away from the road long enough to flash her a grin. "In that case, tell me all about yourself."

He listened to the lull of her voice as she told him about growing up as the daughter of a movie producer who was the equivalent of middle-management, along with a sometimes-actor mother. As she recounted wacky stories of her parents' adventures, he mused that it wasn't a bad way to spend the rest of their drive together. One thing came through to him as she told stories of her life was her lack of involvement in her parents' stories, or her memories of them.

It sounded like she'd been alone a lot, and her self-deprecating comments about being a Plain Jane that she'd made the day of Rudy's surgery came back to haunt him. Had her parents just been too involved in their own lives, or had they deliberately shunned her because she wasn't a classic beauty back then? Unless he met them and had a chance to ask, he supposed he'd never know. It was just one more piece of the puzzle that comprised Shannon Soal.

Chapter Eight

SHANNON DIDN'T REALIZE how boring the cabin would be until the next morning. When they'd arrived, she'd fallen straight into bed in the guest room, not even taking time to hide the phone she had taken from the back of her nightstand. She'd invented a pretext to return to her room last night after hearing about the embargo on her electronics.

It was the emergency phone she kept by her bed in case of a break-in or some other emergency that would necessitate needing a spare quickly at hand if her main phone was charging. It was a basic smartphone included on her plan, and she rarely had occasion to use it. The only person who had the number was Misty, and now she fished it from her bag and quickly sent her friend a text to apprise her of the situation. Shannon was careful not to reveal the location though, because Andre had been adamant about that.

He'd also insisted that she leave behind her electronics, but she simply couldn't be that out of touch for who knew how long. She had patients to check on and had to be able to phone her partners to arrange for them to cover for her for the next week or so.

She crept to the door, once again marveling at how quiet everything was, which probably meant there was nothing to do. The phone was in her hand, and she opened her door just wide enough to try to determine where Andre was. A *thunking* sound caught her attention that seemed to come from outside.

She moved from the door of the guest room to the closest window and peeked through, pausing for a moment to admire the view as Andre sliced a log in two with one strike of a maul.

He was a tempting sight, but she couldn't allow herself to get sidetracked. Her first phone call was to one of the partners, who agreed to cover her rounds and help shuffle her appointments. In parting, she asked, "Do you know how Rudy is?"

"He was released from the hospital this morning, and he's gone home with his foster mother. I assume he'll have a follow-up next week?"

"Yes, on Tuesday." A pang went through her at the idea of missing his appointment. It would be the first time she hadn't seen Rudy for follow-up since he'd become her patient six years ago. She'd pretty much been involved in the process of all of his procedures from beginning to end, at least when they came under the purview of reconstructive surgery.

After hanging up with her partner, who had promised to relay her message to the other partner, she checked her phone and had a response from Misty. As always, her friend was sweetly expressing her concern and admonishing Shannon to stay safe. She appreciated that Misty hadn't pushed to find her location, because she didn't want to lie to her friend.

On the other hand, she couldn't betray Andre any further than sneaking along an unauthorized phone. She didn't have plans to use it for anything besides maintaining contact with her partners and Misty, and it wouldn't matter anyway for long. There were only two bars remaining of the four original ones, and she hadn't had a chance to grab the charger.

After tucking the phone into the back corner of the closet and covering it with her suitcase, Shannon retrieved clothes and went to the only bathroom in the cabin. It had a large stall, and she quickly washed before stepping out to dry off.

As she started to dress, Shannon cursed softly when she realized she had left her underwear behind in her bag. She couldn't still hear chopping sounds, but that could be because she was in the bathroom with the door closed, and it was on the other side of the cabin. With a hesitant look at the towel, she reached for and swathed it around herself, satisfied that it covered everything modestly and wrapped twice around her. The gaudy orange color was off-putting, but she wasn't planning to wear it for more than a minute.

Shannon opened the door and darted into the hallway, so focused on reaching her room that she didn't take a moment to look around her, or she might not have plowed full on into Andre. His hands on her shoulders steadied her, or her bare feet would've caused her to slip on the wood floor.

She looked up into his brown eyes, her heart racing with the adrenaline of nearly falling, combined with being pressed so close to him. "Sorry. I didn't see you."

"It's not a problem. Are you all right?"

She nodded, finding it a bit difficult to make the motion, let alone find more words. It was impossible to move at all, even though she realized—and appreciated—that she was literally pressed against Andre, who was shirtless. Only her towel kept their chests from touching.

He stared at her for half a second before clearing his throat and swinging a wide arc around her. "Let me get out of your way."

She managed a shaky smile and covered the rest of the distance to her room, closing the door behind her and leaning against it as she breathed deeply for a moment. She hadn't wanted him to get out of her way. What she'd yearn for was for him to hold the towel between his fingers and pluck it quickly from her body before leading her into the master bedroom. Or the guest room. She wasn't picky.

Shannon shook her head at her own silliness before moving away from the door to retrieve more clothing. The items waiting in the bathroom would just have to be there until she needed them again, or until she was in there once more. She was actually glad her panties weren't sitting on top, since that would've been embarrassing.

An image of Andre appreciating her underwear, while imagining her wearing it, as he stroked himself, popped into her head. Her cheeks felt hot, and she waved a hand in front of her face to cool down. She couldn't spend all of her time trapped in the cabin fantasizing about Andre.

As she left her room, finding no sign of Andre, she went to the kitchen and started snooping through the fridge and cabinet. Andre had insisted on stopping at a small grocery store twenty miles from the cabin last night, and she was glad he had done so now. They had the basics and more to whip up food, and she quickly started the process for an omelet. As she worked, she looked around the kitchen, finding only two cookbooks and a basic assortment of gadgets and utensils.

After breakfast, she discovered the cabin was equally bare elsewhere. There was a television, but no satellite service. Andre had apologized for not arranging to activate it, but he'd forgotten in the rush. There was a small shelf of books, ranging on topics from how to clean your gun, to self-defense, to a few from a thriller author she didn't recognize, whose pen name was Jason Hollister. Taking a seat on the couch, she grabbed one and started reading.

It was engrossing, but couldn't hold her attention for long. She was restless and antsy, so she set aside the book and went in search of Andre. He wasn't in the cabin, so she cautiously opened the door and stuck out her head. "Andre?" she called.

"In here," he called back from a storage shed nearby.

She stepped out of the cabin and closed the door behind her after ensuring it wasn't locked. Leaves crunched under her feet, and it was a reminder that early fall in the mountains was quite different from early fall in Hollywood. It was beautiful, if completely devoid of anything to actually do.

When she entered the shed, she found Andre stacking the firewood he had cut earlier. "Will we really need that?"

He shrugged as he stood up, dusting his hands down his beat-up jeans. "Probably not, though it's always possible at higher elevations. Fifty degrees up here feels a lot colder than it does in Los Angeles."

"Can I help you?"

He shook his head. "I'm all done."

She let out a sigh. "Is there something I can do? I'm feeling a little antsy here."

"We could go fishing."

She arched her brow. "I can honestly say I've never done that."

He grinned at her. "It's about time to learn then."

FISHING WAS MORE EXCITING than she had expected, though there were still interminable periods of doing nothing while waiting for the fish to bite. In the end, she caught one bass to his two, and they had a feast ready for dinner when they returned to the cleaning station outside the cabin.

"Get the knife in there just like that."

She followed Andre's directions for skinning and filleting the fish with expert motions.

"You're natural at that." He sounded impressed.

She laughed. "I'm a surgeon by trade, and while I've never operated on a fish before, the actual cutting process isn't a lot different."

He clapped a hand on her shoulder. "In that case, your reward for being so good at it is to get to do it every time we catch fish."

She rolled her eyes as she set aside the set of knives and started washing her hands with the faucet and bucket system rigged up outside the house. "What an honor." Inside though, the cockles of her heart warmed as she imagined future trips with Andre to his cabin. It wouldn't be under such terrible circumstances, and they would be free to enjoy each other and fill all the boring times in more interesting ways.

"I'll cook, since you cleaned."

She shrugged as she followed him inside, leaning against the counter. "I'd rather help you. I'm not sure what to do with myself here."

"How about you make the salad and open the wine?"

"That, I can handle."

TWO GLASSES OF WINE, a small fire Andre had built on her prompting (more for atmosphere than for warmth), and the solitude of the night were a dangerous combination, she decided as she swallowed the last sip of her wine. She was thinking thoughts she definitely shouldn't be thinking, starting with wondering how easy it would be to unsnap the faux buttons on Andre's cotton plaid shirt that he'd donned that morning. "Do you come here a lot?"

"Probably two or three times a year. With the Marshals, I didn't have a lot of time, and then when I was in recovery, I wasn't up to visiting this place alone for a while."

She arched her brow. "Alone?"

He nodded. "I hardly ever bring guests here."

"And girlfriends?"

He shook his head after moment, looking like he wasn't sure about answering. "It's kind of my refuge, you know?"

"You brought me here." She leaned forward to place her wineglass on the coaster atop the roughhewn wood table that looked like it had been carved from the complete trunk of a tree.

His glass joined hers, and he leaned back against the sofa with his arm stretched out over the top. It was the perfect position for snuggling, but she wasn't certain if it was an unspoken invitation. "That's different. I need to keep you safe."

"But you wouldn't bring me here if I were your girlfriend?"

He licked his full lips for a moment, not answering.

"Andre?" she prompted.

"I always figured I'd save the cabin for someone special."

It wasn't the answer she wanted. "So I wouldn't be special enough for you to bring here?"

He frowned at her. "Don't be ridiculous."

She shrugged. "I'm not trying to be. I was just curious. What do you think of me, Andre? So many people claim to like me, but it's not really me so much as the celebrity doctor they think I am, and the life they think I lead."

"I think you're special." He reached out and took her hand, though he seemed reluctant to do so. "I absolutely would bring you to the cabin if you were my girlfriend."

She rolled her eyes. "Now you're just saying that to make me feel better."

Andre chuckled. "Can I win this thing?"

In a split-second decision, deciding to ignore the voice of caution, Shannon leaned back against him and snuggled under his arm. "No, I don't think you can."

"In that case, I should probably exercise my right to remain silent."

She held her breath for a moment as she waited to see if he would pull away while trading banter, but he just relaxed with her against him, his arm over her shoulder, and his hand cupping her elbow.

"This is probably dangerous."

She looked around. "Because we're in front of a window?"

He shook his head. "That's good observation though. No, I just meant this closeness. It threatens to distract me."

Shannon looked around again. "In case you haven't noticed, there's nothing much from which to be distracted around here."

"So we should just snuggle to fill the time?"

She wriggled a bit closer, putting her hand on his thigh within a couple of inches of his cock. "Why should we stop with cuddling?" She slid her hand higher, groaning with frustration when his clamped on top of it to keep her from reaching her ultimate goal. "Do you want me, Andre?"

It was his turn to groan. "Of course I do. This is just a bad idea since you're my client, and I'm responsible for your safety."

"I trust you completely to keep me safe, but that isn't what I need most right now. What I really need in this moment is you." She held her breath after making the admission, hating to leave herself so vulnerable and exposed, but feeling the need to make sure Andre understood exactly what she wanted.

Apparently, her message came through loud and clear, because he shifted on the couch until he lifted her onto his lap, which brought their heads nearly level. He bent just the slightest bit, and she stretched upward a tad so that their lips could meet. He kissed her thoroughly, his tongue dipping into her mouth within seconds of their lips touching. Hers reached out to return the strokes, and she was relieved neither one of them were shy lovers. Apparently, he'd decided to give her what she wanted with his full enthusiasm.

She trailed a hand down his flannel shirt, testing for herself how easy it was to unsnap the faux buttons with one hand. It proved to be a cinch, and he was soon bare-chested, allowing full access for her eager hand. She stroked up and down the expanse, running her fingers lightly through his crisp smattering of hair before gently tracing some of the older-looking scars. She knew they were all from the same injury, but some had healed faster than others, not being as deep.

One of his scars led to the pubic hair peeking up from his cock, so she let her fingers roam down the waistband of his jeans.

He suddenly pulled away, breaking the kiss. "This is a damned inconvenient place for this. Let's go to bed."

Shannon beamed at him as she hopped off his lap. "That's a terrific idea. Which room?"

"Mine. I have a king-size bed in there, and it's just waiting for you, Dr. Soal."

"Ohh, how formal. Do you like calling me Dr. Soal under the circumstances?"

Andre smacked her on the butt, urging her to hurry down the hallway. "It's equal parts thrilling and terrifying, to be honest."

She stopped in the doorway, spinning to face him as his seriousness caught her attention. "What do you mean, terrifying?"

He shrugged a shoulder. "It's just that you're so smart and talented, and it's a little intimidating. I'm just an old, scarred, retired U.S. Marshal."

She made a scoffing sound. "You're hardly old, and you're still in the protection business. As for the scars, they don't bother me in the least. I have my own."

He looked skeptical, so Shannon leaned closer to him, pointing out the fine white lines along her jaw, behind her ear, and across her nose. "Those are from the surgeries that restored my face. Even the best plastic surgeon can't completely prevent scarring, but makeup covers it easily."

He still seemed hesitant, but took her hand when she grabbed his and led him into his room. "This is a lot for anyone to take in." He gestured to his stomach.

She shrugged. "I'm a doctor, and I've seen worse."

"Seeing and interacting are two different things."

With a sigh of annoyance, she put her hands on her hips. "Are you going to make me prove it to you?" At his look of confusion, she dropped to her knees with a melodramatic sigh. "I guess you are." She leaned closer to him, extending her tongue to run it down the first scar closest to her. He let out a breath that sounded almost like a sizzling sound through his teeth, and his entire body jerked against her.

He put a hand in her hair. "You don't have to do that to prove a point, Shannon."

She pulled away from his stomach just briefly. "I'm doing it because I want to." Then she returned to her quest, tracing all the lines and angles from his injury outward and downward. Soon enough, her exploration drifted from his scars to his cock pressing insistently against the denim. He groaned in what sounded like relief when she popped the snap and unzipped his pants, pulling them down to his thighs along with his red briefs.

He was thick and long, with a slight curve to the left, and a bead of pre-cum dripped from the tip. She leaned forward to catch it on her tongue, closing her eyes as she gently wrapped her mouth around his shaft and slowly took him in. Andre was stiff against her, in more ways than one, and his hand in her hair clutched desperately as he cradled the back of her head, though he didn't try to force her to stay in that position.

Shannon ran her tongue up and down the length of him, tracing the veiny sides, before focusing her attention on the underside at the sensitive vee. He seemed to particularly like it when she flicked her tongue across that, so she applied more pressure with the broadside of her tongue, making his hips buck and eliciting a groan from him.

She bobbed her head, drawing in her cheeks to suck as hard as she could as she moved up and down his shaft, wanting him to come with the same level of need that seemed to pour off him in waves. She could tell he was getting there, so she cradled his balls and gently massaged them as she squeezed the base of his shaft, where her mouth wouldn't reach.

He hovered on the edge, but she was the one who cried out when he suddenly wrenched away. Still on her knees, she frowned up at him as he turned away for a moment, breathing deeply. "Did I do something wrong?" She hadn't had any complaints from anyone else, but clearly something had taken him out of the moment.

He shook his head as he turned back to her, his hand going to her hair once again, this time in a stroking motion. "You were too good. I just don't want to blow it yet. I'd rather go with you than before you."

She exhaled with relief and took his hand as he helped her to her feet. "In that case, I guess I have some catching up to do." She pulled her long-sleeve shirt over her head and tossed it carelessly toward the trunk at the foot of the bed. His gaze was focused on her as she reached behind her to unsnap her bra and slowly slid it off, an inch at a time.

The black satin garment joined the T-shirt in roughly the same vicinity, and her hands moved to her hips. She'd worn yoga pants, so there was no need to unfasten anything. She simply hooked her thumbs in the waistband and pulled them down along with her underwear.

Shannon was glad she had left her shoes at the back door when they come in from fishing, so she didn't have to deal with that awkwardness, unlike poor Andre. It made her want to giggle for a moment as he shifted and looked like he might fall before reaching out to brace a palm against the wall so he could kick off his sneakers and finish removing his clothes.

Then it was just the two of them, naked together, and nothing separating them except a few inches of space.

They reached for each other simultaneously, and her arm slid around his waist as his enfolded her upper back. Shannon snuggled against Andre for a moment, just enjoying the sensations evoked from the simple touch. Of course it wasn't enough to keep them sated for long, and having him so close, and so explorable, increased her desire.

With clasped hands, they moved to the bed, lying down on their sides to face each other. Andre leaned forward to kiss her at the same time he lifted one of her thighs to move her leg across his hip. It opened her to his questing fingers, and they soon slid into her slick heat.

Shannon closed her eyes and bit back a cry of pleasure as he started to stroke her clit in almost the same rhythm that his tongue was moving across hers in her mouth. She was wetter than she could ever remember being, and she wanted him right then. When his finger drifted lower, seeking out the bundle of nerves just below her clit that made her so sensitive, she almost jumped off the bed, and he laughed.

"Don't go anywhere yet." With those words, Andre flipped her position so that he was lying on top of her, her thigh still around his hip, her other leg splayed outward. It was now his thumb caressing her, bringing her closer to the edge of orgasm with every sensuous stroke, and she trembled as she struggled to fight it.

"Let yourself go, Shannon."

She shook her head, squeezing her eyes closed tightly.

"Why not?"

"You want to come with me, not before me. I feel the same way." When she opened her eyes, it was to find his burning intensely, and the hunger she saw stoked her own.

"In that case, let's go together." His hand moved away from her, and though it was what she'd requested, she still had to fight back the urge to protest the loss of the sensations. A moment later, the bedside drawer squeaked, and he winced. "I forgot to bring WD-40. It's been a while since this drawer's seen any action."

"I thought you didn't bring girlfriends here?"

He looked sheepish. "Which is why the drawer squeaks from disuse. I still keep condoms here though. It's just sensible."

She laughed as he withdrew a strip of condoms, taking one from him and tearing open the foil packet. Shannon locked her gaze with his as she smoothed the latex down his cock, preparing him to enter her.

Her hand remained on his shaft, guiding him to her core, and she gasped lightly when he started to enter her. It had been a while since her last relationship, and Andre's size made him a challenge for even the most experienced woman. But she was wet and ready, and he finally slid inside after a moment's resistance, and there was no more pain.

She clutched his shoulders and wrapped her thighs around his hips as he cupped her buttocks in his hands and dragged her closer. The rhythm was slow to start with, as he learned her inner terrain, and she continued to adjust to his generous size. Soon enough, all hints of exploration disappeared, and they started thrusting frantically together, needing to come, and hoping to do it together.

Shannon could feel herself hovering on the edge, but she wasn't quite there when Andre's cock tightened, and the first small spasms spread through him.

"Just a minute." Was that raspy voice really hers? She slid her hand between them, moving her fingers to her clit to stroke herself until the pleasure that had been building in her womb spread outward, and she started to convulse around the cock filling her so perfectly.

Andre let go then too, his convulsions merging with hers, until was difficult to tell who was trembling with release. It was both of them, and it was more than physical. As he collapsed against her a moment later, before turning them onto their sides to prevent burying her under his weight, she laid her head against his chest and listened to his still-racing heartbeat. The rhythm lulled her into sleep, and she slept more soundly than she had in months.

Chapter Nine

ANDRE STILL WASN'T sure he had done the right thing as he slid out of bed early the next morning. Shannon was still curled up on her stomach and sleeping deeply, so he left her to it. He'd rested like the dead himself for a while, but now that he was awake, he was fully awake. He was rarely able to go back to sleep for that reason.

A glance at the clock revealed it was seven-thirty, but he was still quiet as he took a shower and started coffee. His phone from Olivia rang at eight-oh-two, and he answered it when he recognized Jared's phone number that he'd programmed in yesterday. "Hello?"

"The bastard's escalated again."

"What did he do?" A chill went through Andre as he imagined the possibilities.

"He knows she's gone, and he's demanding she return. He accused her of ripping out his heart by walking away, and he told her he'd do the same if she didn't come back. Then he left her a gift."

"What kind of gift?"

"A heart with a knife through it."

"A real heart?" asked Andre with a hint of disbelief.

"It's just a pig's heart, but it's still chilling."

"How do you know it's a pig's heart?"

"It's too small to be an adult's, and it's definitely not human anyway, according to one of the patrol cops who was at the scene. He grew up on a pig farm, apparently."

"I'll be glad to get the test results confirming his opinion, but I'm relieved it's not a human heart."

"No, but it's definitely frightening. She must be terrified, or she will be when you tell her."

"Maybe you should send me some pictures or something, so I can use it to convince her if she's in disbelief." Andre had no intention of showing any such images to Shannon, but he was suddenly plagued by the need to know that the event had actually occurred.

"No can do. Those are still being developed, and the heart's with the lab now."

"I see." Andre paused for a moment before letting out a deep breath. "You're pretty wrapped up in this case. How well do you know Shannon?"

"You've already asked me that. Are you afraid I'll steal her from you?" asked Silver with a laugh. It sounded forced though.

"Not at all. I was just curious how well you knew her?"

"I don't know. As well as anyone, I guess. I met her about a year ago, and we saw each other a few times, but it wasn't social. I liked her, and when I saw her name appear on the list of new cases, I scooped it up."

That explained the coincidence then, but it still didn't completely get Silver off the hook. If he'd wanted a way in to Shannon's life, what better means than to create a stalker from whom he could rescue her? "Are you in love with Shannon?"

"That's a ballsy question. Are you, Hart?"

He looked up then at a sound in the doorway, finding a fresh-faced Shannon just out of the shower, with damp hair hanging around her face. "You know, I'm not sure that I'm not." He didn't wait for a reply as he hung up, knowing he wasn't going to get Jared to admit he was the stalker if that was the case. Andre didn't want to become fixated on it either, in case the detective wasn't the person terrorizing Shannon.

As she moved closer, the concern in her expression weighed heavily on him. "I heard some of that. My stalker left me a heart?"

He nodded. "It's nothing to be afraid of though. You're safe here."

"Yeah, sure." She sounded unconvinced for a moment as she padded to the table on bare feet and took a seat. "What if he finds me here? And if he doesn't, I can't stay here forever. What do I do if they can't find him this week? Or next week? I can't be in limbo like this, just waiting, and hiding out in this cabin."

He moved to the table, taking a seat beside her to take her hand. "You can stay as long as you need to, and as long as it's keeping you safe, I want you to be here. I know you want to get back to your regular life, but you have to be patient. I'm sure he won't find you here, so as long as you sit tight and give Silver a chance to work, this nightmare should end soon."

Her gaze was haunted, but she looked like she was clinging to hope. "Do you really think so?"

He brought her hand to his mouth, brushing his lips against the knuckles. "I certainly do. I intend to make it my top priority." Making her happy, even if it meant she wouldn't need him as a bodyguard anymore, was his paramount goal.

He had worried that getting close to the doctor would be dangerous and that it might upset his focus, but now he was utterly calm and could view the situation with razor precision. If he was the only thing standing between Shannon and her stalker, he wouldn't get careless or distracted. He cared too much about her to allow that to happen.

Having sex with her hadn't been a mistake. It'd simply forced him to acknowledge the emotions growing between them and had enhanced his determination to protect her. And since it wasn't a mistake... "Are you hungry? If not, you might want to go back to bed for a while." He waggled his eyebrows in a suggestive manner to let her know exactly what he was proposing. He hoped it would distract her from her heavy thoughts.

Her expression was conflicted for a moment, remaining tense for another half-second before she allowed herself to relax. It was clear she was mentally switching gears to focus on the here-and-now with him rather than the horrible "gift" her stalker left her.

"I could wait a while to eat." She was giggling as they rushed from the table to the bedroom, and she jumped on the bed. He joined her a moment later, thrilled to hear her laughs of delight that replaced the fear in her eyes and the despondency in her voice from a few moments before.

Chapter Ten

SHANNON WOKE IN THE middle of the night, uncertain what had disturbed her for a moment. She was still lying beside Andre in the bed, the place she had occupied for the last three nights, and she had slept like a baby for all of them until now.

"What is it, Jared?"

The murmur of Andre's voice alerted her to the fact that he was speaking on the phone, and she assumed the ring was what woke her. Her stomach clenched with nerves as she turned on her side to better hear the conversation, since Andre didn't put it on speakerphone.

"The stalker... Attacked... Misty... Hospital."

Shannon sat upright as she gleaned those words, staring pointedly at the phone and catching Andre's attention. She mimed he should put it on speakerphone, and he did with a small sigh.

"Please say that again, Detective Silver," she said, once Andre had tapped the speakerphone button. "I didn't get to hear the first part of the conversation."

He sounded startled when he replied. "I didn't expect you to be there for a phone call this late at night."

"What about Misty?" She had no time for other topics of discussion.

After a brief hesitation, he said, "I was just telling Andre that the stalker attacked earlier tonight. He cornered Misty near her apartment building, hit her on the head, and left her."

"Oh my god, where is she?"

"She's still in the hospital, but the ER staff doesn't expect to keep her all night, so I've offered her my spare room tonight for after she's discharged. The stalker stole her purse, which had her car keys, house keys, identification, and phone inside. We suspect he attacked Misty to get the phone, so he might be able to get hold of you, but she's afraid to go home, and who can blame her? That's why she's staying with me tonight, in my spare room. It's strictly platonic."

Shannon shook her head, not caring about that last part, and certainly having no jealousy about her friend staying with him. His assurance that it was platonic was unnecessary. Another time, she would have to be blunt about her disinterest. "Did she get a look at him?"

"She described him as big and bulky, but didn't see his face. He didn't give her a chance to fully turn around."

She cursed under her breath. "I'm going to call her to see how she's doing."

"I Imagine she'd like that."

"Is that the only development, Detective Silver?" asked Andre.

"Yeah, for now. There've been a few more letters delivered, with each one growing angrier that she's slipped away, but nothing else has happened between the heart with a knife and Misty's attack, except for those."

"Thank you for keeping us apprised."

When Andre hung up the phone, Shannon snatched it out of his hand without asking. He looked annoyed, but didn't try to stop her as she called the number for the hospital from memory and requested to be put through to Misty's room. As a courtesy, she put it on speakerphone for Andre to hear too. Her friend answered midway through the second ring.

"Hello?" She sounded raspy, and there was a drugged quality to her voice.

"Misty, it's Shannon. I just heard what happened. Are you all right?" Tears streamed from her eyes as she asked the question, and she appreciated when Andre reached over and dabbed at her cheeks with a tissue.

"I feel awful. He rammed my head into the side of my car, and he was really angry, Shannon. He's demanding you come back, or he'll keep hurting people. He told me he'd kill me the next time he had to come for me." Misty started sobbing.

"It's okay. I'm coming back."

Andre snatched the phone from her fingers. "Misty, you know I can't bring her back. It isn't safe."

"I know, but I'm just so scared."

"Stay with Jared, and he'll protect you." He hesitated for a moment. "Better yet, don't stay with Jared. Go visit some other friends, or stay with your family."

She sounded confused. "I don't have any family, and what's wrong with the detective?"

Andre looked like he didn't want to tell her, but he finally sighed and said, "I'm a little suspicious of him. He has too much interest in Shannon, and he knew her before the stalking began. I think it'd be better all-around if you stayed somewhere else besides his home."

"Okay." She hiccupped. "What do I do if he comes back?"

"Jared?"

"No, the stalker. He's going to kill me if he can't get to Shannon."

"I'd suggest you take it few days off as well, at least until we catch this guy. Don't go back to your apartment."

"Use your company credit card to check in somewhere like a spa for a few days," said Shannon as loudly as she could, so her friend could hear her since Andre had taken the phone and refused to give it back.

"I guess that would be fun. I think I'll go to that place in Mendocino. Do you remember it, Shannon?"

Shannon hoped the smile was audible in her voice. "We had a heck of a girls' weekend. That sounds like a clever idea, and I know you'll still be safe there and out of harm's way."

"Okay, that's what I'll do. They're going to release me tonight. I'll stay with someone besides the detective, and then I'm going to the spa."

Andre hung up the phone a moment later, and Shannon glared at him. "I need to go back."

He shook his head. "No way. You're safe here. The deed is still registered in my maternal uncle's name, so there's no link to me and the property. Your stalker would have to physically comb the mountains to find you here. This is the only place you're safe, and I won't risk your safety. You can't leave here until we find him."

She crossed her arms over her chest. "He's going to go after the people I care about. What about my partners and their families? I have friends, patients, and a few cousins nearby. If he finds a link to any of those people, they're at risk. You can't guard them all."

"And you can't sacrifice yourself to save them. You're not turning yourself over to your stalker, and that's final."

"It isn't your call to make."

Andre's expression hardened. "Yes, it is. I have the keys to the Jeep, and I'm not letting you leave." His voice softened. "I'm not trying to be a hard ass, and I'm certainly not trying to control you, but you aren't thinking rationally. Right now, you're ready to head off half-cocked to save everyone, and you don't even know if they're at risk."

"Misty was at risk."

He nodded. "Yes, but she was an obvious target. She's been on the show off and on, and everyone knows she's your assistant. I'll call Jared back and have him assign protection duty for other obvious targets, like your partners and their families, but you aren't going back there yet."

She slid out of bed and stood up, too angry to care that she was naked, and currently uninterested in sex with him. She marched across the room.

"Where are you going, Shannon?"

"To the guest room. I assume I'm still allowed to go there?"

"If you prefer, of course you can sleep there, but I'd rather have you beside me."

She stumbled for a moment, hand on the doorknob. Shannon softened her voice slightly when she looked back at him, losing some of the snark. "I just need some time to process everything. I'm really angry right now, and I don't want to say something I'll regret."

He looked reluctant to let her leave, but he didn't try to stop her when she opened the door and stepped through, closing it behind her. Shannon padded down the wooden floor on her bare feet, shaking with chills by the time she reached the guest room. She took a moment to fish the phone from the back of the closet before burrowing under the covers on the smaller guest bed. It wasn't nearly as comfortable as the one she'd been sharing with Andre, but she couldn't lie beside him right now without exchanging acrimonious words.

She might understand his perspective, and perhaps she'd even appreciate his protectiveness if it wasn't putting others at risk, but she thought he was making a mistake. Coming to the cabin had probably been a bad idea from the beginning, and even if she was safe there, she couldn't leave her friends vulnerable if she could stop the stalker from attacking another one. Already, Misty had fallen victim to whomever wanted to hurt her, and the guilt lacerated her insides. If she hadn't left, Misty wouldn't have been injured.

As she lay there, her anger grew, but it wasn't directed toward Andre. It was focused solely on her stalker, whom she hated with a passion. How dare he destroy her life in this fashion? She hadn't done anything to him and had certainly never provoked his attention. Why her? She was nothing special in the scheme of things, and she hoped she finally would get an explanation for the stalker's fixation once they caught him. It just made no sense to her.

Chapter Eleven

SHE HAD FALLEN ASLEEP holding the phone, and the muffled beep from a text message woke her. Shannon blinked open her eyes and looked down at the phone, which was down to its very last bar. Recognizing Misty's number made her heart seize with fear, since she knew her friend didn't have the phone any longer. Her fingers trembled when she opened the text message, and she let out a sharp gasp at the sight.

The very first thing she saw was a picture of Rudy with a knife over his head. The little boy was asleep and completely unaware of the mortal danger that threatened him. Anger and fear warred for supremacy inside her, and she would have lashed out with her bare hands against the stalker if he'd been in the same room with her.

A text message came next, and it was succinct. If she didn't meet her admirer, as he described himself, at the included address by one o'clock, he would kill Rudy.

Before she could reply, the phone died. Shannon let out a small moan of fear, unable to recall the address for a long moment. Finally, it popped into her head, and she rolled out of bed to search frantically among her things for piece of paper and a pen.

She had to settle for an eyeliner pencil, but it was legible on the back of the receipt she found tucked in her wallet. She wrote down the address before she could forget it and then stared at it for a long moment.

She didn't know what to do. Andre would never agree to her meeting the stalker, but she was terrified to go alone. Without her phone, she couldn't confirm that Rudy was in any danger, and she doubted Andre would follow up to ensure he wasn't. Even if he did, and they discovered Rudy was missing, he wouldn't let her meet with the stalker. That was clear after last night's argument.

Risking Rudy was unacceptable, and though she knew it was a poor choice to acquiesce to her stalker's demands, Shannon decided it was the only one available to her.

She dressed quickly and moved to her door, opening it to listen for Andre. The shower was running, and relief filled her. She crept down the hallway with her boots in her hand and eased open the door to Andre's room. She had watched him undress for the last three nights, and he was meticulous about storing his wallet, keys, and phone in the top dresser drawer. She opened it and was disappointed to find the phone gone, since she could have used it to call Rudy's foster mother and ascertain if the boy was missing. The keys were a welcome sight though, and she scooped them up to depart, running through the house as quietly she could on socked feet.

In the kitchen, Shannon paused for a moment in front of the whiteboard hanging on the refrigerator. She erased the list of needed supplies to make room to leave Andre a note. She tried to be brief with her correspondence, but left the address at the bottom. She might be doing a stupid thing, but she wasn't stupid enough to run off without letting him know where she was heading. It would take him a couple of hours to get a ride back to the city, so he wouldn't be able to stop her from meeting her stalker, but maybe he would arrive about the same time as the meeting hour.

She left the house and got into the Jeep, starting it up. As she started to reverse, the door to the cabin opened, and Andre ran out. Even in the moment, she couldn't fail to appreciate the sleek lines of his wet body, and it was obvious he'd run straight from the shower.

He was calling her name and waving his arms, and she paused for just a moment. She stared at him for a half-second, shook her head, and then continued backing down the driveway. She couldn't look back as she turned at the end to emerge onto the road. If she did, she might not maintain the resolve to keep going, and she couldn't risk leaving Rudy to the stalker's mercy.

Chapter Twelve

SHE ARRIVED BACK IN the city a couple of hours before the designated meeting time, and at first didn't know what to do with herself. Then it occurred to her that maybe she could sneak into the building and at least get a lay of the land before the stalker showed up. If she were really lucky, she might find Rudy there—and just Rudy.

Before making her way to the address, she stopped at a convenience store and bought a disposable cell phone. It took a few minutes to hook up the service, but then she was able to call Rudy's parents' house. There was no answer at the foster parents', and that sent a chill through her.

Next, she called Jared, who sounded angry when he answered. "What the hell are you doing?"

Shannon frowned. "Do I have the wrong number?"

"This is Shannon, isn't it? It's an unknown number, but I figured it had to be you."

She took a sharp breath. "Yes, it's me. I need you to check out something for me."

"What? How insane you are to run off on your own?"

Andre had ratted her out. "Can you please see if Rudy's foster parents have reported him missing?"

"Is Rudy the kid your stalker threatened?"

"How did you know about that?" She abruptly recalled Andre's warning to Misty to not stay with Jared last night, and suspicion filled her. "What would make you ask that?"

"Because that's what Andre told me when he called a while ago to warn me that you were about to do something stupid. Don't go to that address."

"I have to. I have to know if Rudy's in there, and I really need to end this thing."

"You're going to end up dead. Have some common sense."

"You know where to find me, and at what time. Be there." She hung up before Jared could further advise her to be sensible. She was completely aware of how bad this decision was, but none of them seemed to understand how driven she was to protect Rudy. It was a strong instinct that she couldn't ignore, as though he were her child, and the mother bear instinct had kicked into full gear.

The phone rang a minute later, and she wouldn't have answered it, except she hadn't gotten a reply from Jared about whether Rudy was missing. "Hello?"

"There have been no missing persons' reports filed, but there's no one at the Johnstons' home. I really can't tell you for sure either way, Shannon. I'm begging you not to go in there alone though. Wait for me or Andre."

"Andre's a bit behind me."

"He'll be here soon. His friend in the NSA sent him a chopper."

"Oh, that's good news." Probably. She wanted him with her, but knew he was going to be pissed.

She pulled up a half a block away from the designated meeting spot, wincing at the decrepit area around her. It'd once been a thriving industrial park, but it was now little more than crumbling heaps of concrete and metal. "I have to go in to see if Rudy's there. Come find me, Jared, and send Andre too."

After hanging up the phone, she slid it into her pocket, and then put Andre's keys in her other pocket. After sliding out of the Jeep, which she locked with the fob, she took a couple of steps before realizing she couldn't go in without any kind of weapon. That would be even more foolhardy than her already-set course before her.

She turned back to the Jeep and unlocked it, going around the back to search for something she could use for a weapon. She settled on the tire iron, which felt substantial in her hand, and then locked the vehicle again and slowly approached the spot where she was supposed to meet her stalker.

The address was about the only thing left that was recognizable. A good section of the wall was missing, and the roof seemed like it had caved in long ago. She looked around, searching for someone's presence, but seeing nothing obvious. Nor could she figure out how to get into the building since the doorway was blocked.

She walked around the side of the building, and there was a more intact door there, but the wall around it was almost completely gone. It afforded a full glimpse of most of the interior, and it appeared to be deserted. Had she remembered the address incorrectly? The thought made her heart seize in her chest, and it took a moment to resume beating. No, she was certain she had written down the correct numbers, but there was nowhere to actually meet here.

Still confused and trying to puzzle it out, she walked back around to the front of the building. Movement from the corner of her eye caught her attention, but she couldn't turn her head in time to see what was happening. A second later, something solid collided with her temple, and unconsciousness immediately overtook her.

SHANNON WAS SLOW TO wake up, and when she did, it hurt to open her eyes. She soon figured out the reason was because of the bright light shining down on her. It was focused right on her, and it was blinding in its brilliance. It was even worse than some of the lights they used while filming the reality show.

She blinked and tried to lift a hand to her eyes to shield them, but discovered her hands were tied behind her back. She was seated in a chair, her legs bound to it, and there was nothing but cement floor and walls all around her. "Where am I?" Her voice sounded raspy, and she wondered how long she had been passed out.

"Right where I intended you to be all along, Shannon."

Shannon's stomach threatened to expel its contents when she recognized the voice. A chill went down her spine, and she shook her head before a flash of pain reminded her that was a bad idea. The entire left side of her head throbbed as she did so.

"It hurts, doesn't it?" The voice feigned sympathy. "It hurt like a bitch when I slammed my head into the car to really sell the story, but I knew I had to do it. After all the other pain you caused me, it was just one brief incident necessary to get my hands on you."

"Why are you doing this, Misty?"

At the sound of her name, the woman she had thought was her friend and assistant stepped into the light, but off to the side. She wore a bulky outfit, and Shannon recognized it is the same one the stalker had worn at the gala when she tried to snatch her. It couldn't really be Misty, could it? "Is he making you do this?"

Misty laughed, but it was a cold and heartless sound. "No one's making me do anything. I do this because I want to. Because you deserve it."

There was a scraping sound of something like metal against cement, and Shannon at first wanted to know what it was. It was only when Misty dragged a tray of instruments on a metal stand into the light that she realized she didn't want to know. It was better not knowing that Misty, who seemed unbalanced, had an arsenal of surgical equipment at the ready. She hoped Jared or Andre showed up soon.

A sinking sensation filled her when she realized Misty had probably moved her. The address she had left for Andre was meaningless now. Misty had outwitted her. "Is Rudy okay?"

Misty looked down at the tray before her, selecting a sharp scalpel and testing the edge of it with a wince as it split her finger. "That's really sharp. It should do nicely."

Shannon squeezed back tears that tried to fall from her eyes. "What have you done to Rudy?"

"That little freak is just fine. The picture was from his recent hospital stay. He never knew I was there. This morning, I stopped by his parents' house to give them all-day passes to Disneyland, courtesy of Dr. Shannon. They were all so grateful, though you couldn't pay me to take him out in public."

Shannon glared at her. "He was born with a birth defect. He could hardly help that."

Misty shrugged. "Sometimes death is the better option. Not in my case though. My baby was just fine. He was healthy and normal, and we had already named him Caleb."

"Caleb?" The name meant nothing to her.

"Caleb Daniel Matheson." She screamed the name.

Shannon shook her head again, wincing at the pain. "I don't know who that is."

"Here's another name for you. Daniel Matheson."

The name sounded familiar, but she couldn't place it. "I don't know—"

"Melissa Matheson?"

"No, I'm sorry."

"How about Anthony Bell?" she screamed.

Shannon froze at that name. "That was my boyfriend. He's been dead for years."

"I know. The careless little bastard got behind the wheel drunk, and you were just as drunk as he was. You went out joyriding, and you cost me everything."

Shannon's mouth went dry as the pieces started to fit together. "We hit a car. I was thrown clear of the accident, but my face was heavily damaged."

"And Bell died a fiery death trapped in that car." She wore ghastly smile. "He got a tenth of the justice he deserved, but you walked away scot-free."

Shannon frowned. "I don't understand. I know you were hurt, but neither one of you were killed. Anthony was the only one who died in the accident."

"And Caleb." Misty suddenly cleared the instrument tray as she punched it. "You killed my baby. He was twenty-eight weeks along and absolutely perfect until the trauma from the accident ripped the placenta from my body. He died before we ever reached the hospital, and I hemorrhaged so badly, they had to do a hysterectomy. My husband left me a year later, unable to be with a woman who couldn't have kids. He didn't want to adopt, and neither did I. I just wanted my perfect little Caleb."

Shannon's mouth was dry, and guilt swept through her all over again. She had made a bad decision as a teenager, not speaking up when Anthony had insisted on driving. She had been drinking as well, so she shouldn't have been behind the wheel either. She should have insisted they both get a ride with someone else, or she should've stayed behind at the party and not gone with Anthony. She hadn't been strong enough to stand up to him at that point, and disaster had been the result.

When it came to Misty, apparently she'd made a series of bad decisions, because she had put herself in the other woman's hands. At least Rudy was safe, but there was no rescue coming for her, since no one knew where she was.

She started tugging at the ropes on her hands, hoping for a weak spot. "You have to know it was an accident. I'm so sorry for what happened your son, and your marriage, but neither Anthony nor I intended for anything awful happened. He's dead, and it's in the past."

"It's not in the past. I live with it every day. I look in the mirror every day and see a barren woman who wasn't good enough for her husband. I think of little Caleb every day, and I ruminate. I've grown very bitter, and a few years ago, I realized there was still one person who had never paid for my suffering. I started looking for you, and it wasn't an easy task.

"You have a different face now, but once I made that connection, it wasn't difficult to discern you were a hotshot plastic surgeon in Hollywood about to get a reality show. It was the perfect opening to insinuate myself into your life and start slowly terrorizing you. Melissa Matheson became Misty Daniels, the quintessential assistant and ideal friend. I wanted to be close to see you suffer as much as I have. I don't think that's actually possible, but we're going to see how much you can take."

She appeared to have calmed down again, and Misty bent down to pick up implements she had scattered with her temper fit, placing them back on the tray with chilling precision. When she stood up, she gave Shannon a bright smile. "I'm afraid they won't be sterile now, but I guess it doesn't matter. Dying from an infection will be the least of your worries."

Shannon tensed, still fighting against her bonds as Misty drew closer, scraping the metal tray against the cement, as though using it to exacerbate Shannon's fear. It was working. "Why now? Why didn't you do this months ago?"

"First, I wanted to watch you squirm before giving you what you deserve. I didn't expect Andre, whose presence accelerated my timeline a bit."

Shannon eyed the tray of instruments as it stopped near her, with Misty a couple of feet away. "What about Andre?"

Misty shrugged. "I expected you to hire a security guard or something, but I didn't expect you to fall for him. It just makes this so much better. I almost decided to send him the new address where I brought you, but in the end, this is about you and me. While I would've loved to kill him while you're watching, before starting in on you, I was afraid I couldn't handle both of you. If I have to choose, you're the obvious blight to remove from this world."

Shannon let out a sob that was partly fear, but also a bit of hope. The bonds at her wrist were starting to stretch and growing slick with her blood, which might help ease her hands through the bindings. Maybe she could find a way to escape before Misty went to work with the surgical instruments. "What do you want to do to me?"

"I thought we would start by trying to give you back your old face. That new one is far too kind and generous. It's flawless. Practically angelic, and we both know you're no angel. You're a drunk driving murderer."

"I was the passenger, not the driver. I should've stopped him, but even if I hadn't ridden with him, he still probably would've gotten behind the wheel. Anthony was stubborn like that. It wouldn't have changed anything, whether or not I was there."

"That's not correct. It would've changed your fate. If you hadn't been complicit with him, you wouldn't be here now. It's time you face some consequences for your actions, Dr. Soal."

"I'm a good person. I've done so much for my patients, and for you, Misty. I thought you were my friend."

"A guilty conscience has a way of making one feel reformed with the slightest good deed. Fixing a bunch of freaks won't bring back my perfect little boy, will it?"

"I can help you find a surrogate. It could be your own egg, even if you couldn't carry the baby." She was frantically tugging at the ropes now, ignoring the pain as best she could as it sliced through the tender skin of her wrists.

"It was a total hysterectomy," yelled Misty right in her face. "They took everything from me to save my life, but it would have been kinder to let me die. You and your boyfriend took everything that mattered."

"I'm so sorry. This isn't going to fix that though."

Misty shrugged. "Nothing will fix it, but at least Caleb will finally have some justice."

"This is revenge, not justice."

Lifting a scalpel, Misty ran it down Shannon's upper arm. "I don't see much of a difference from my perspective."

She cried out as the blade sliced through skin. It was sharp and sure, going deep into the tissue, but not quite reaching the bone.

Misty leaned closer and tsked her tongue. "I didn't realize how deep it would go. I'll have to be more careful. I don't want you exsanguinating too quickly, Dr. Soal. I'd like this to last for several hours. At least thirteen."

Shannon gritted her teeth, still pulling on her ropes. "Why thirteen hours?"

"Because that's how long I had to labor to deliver my dead child."

Shannon frowned. "But you had a hysterectomy. Didn't they do a C-section too?"

Misty frowned, pausing for a moment. Then she laughed. "How silly of me. That was with Marie, my little freak." There was a strange mix of affection and revulsion in her tone.

Shannon's head was spinning, and she wasn't certain if it was from Misty changing the conversation topic quickly, or if it was from the head injury. "Who's Marie?"

"She was my little girl. She was born still at twenty-one weeks due to a chromosomal abnormality. It took thirteen hours to bring her into the world, and I'm sure that's how long it would've taken to birth Caleb. He was my reward for getting through that hell. He wasn't a freak. He was perfect, and he wasn't going to be stillborn. Until you killed him, there was absolutely nothing wrong with him." In a fit of rage, Misty slammed the scalpel into Shannon shoulder and twisted it. "That's right, scream for me."

Shannon wanted to deny her the pleasure, but she'd never felt such horrible pain in all her life. When Misty pulled out the scalpel a moment later, her shoulder was numb, yet throbbing with agony. Her first fear was she would no longer be able to perform surgery.

About that moment, the first set of ropes on her wrist started to give way. She let out another sob of relief, but Misty didn't seem to notice the change in pitch.

"Put down the scalpel and back away from her."

Shannon and Misty both stiffened at the familiar voice, and she peered over Misty's shoulder to see Andre standing in the perimeter of the light with his pistol extended. "How did you find me?" Shannon gasped in relief.

"I kept losing my keys, so I got one of those tags you could put on objects to track where they end up. When you weren't at the designated location, I activated the service and found your address here." As he spoke, his attention remained on Misty, as did his gun. "Step away from her now, Misty."

"No, I don't think so. I've waited too long for this." Misty reached for a fresh scalpel and moved behind Shannon, bringing it to her throat. "She's going to die, loverboy. And you get to watch. I'd rather it be the other way around, and I would've liked to have hours with Shannon, but I'll take what I can get."

Shannon's hand slipped free, and it was the opposite shoulder that hadn't been stabbed. Misty wasn't expecting it, so she was able to elbow her in the solar plexus, sending the other woman reeling backward to land hard on the cement floor.

Andre rushed toward her, reaching into his pocket as he went to pull out a handkerchief. He passed it to Shannon on the way, and it was only then she realized the scalpel had nicked her neck. It wasn't a deep cut, but she was bleeding freely, so she pressed the cloth to it with her working hand.

Her feet were still bound to the chair, so she couldn't stand up, but she was able to scrape it slightly around to get a better view of what was happening.

Misty tried to put up a fight, slashing at Andre with the scalpel she still held, but he managed to successfully block each attempt. He grabbed her wrist and forced her to drop the scalpel just as the sound of running feet filled the building.

A moment later, Detective Silver and six uniformed police officers burst into the room, dislodging the spotlight and sending it spinning to the side. It must have been clipped on something, and it hit the floor with a crash before darkness enveloped them.

"She's loose," said Andre a moment later.

Shannon felt her before Misty reached her. It was something in the way the air changed, or perhaps her primitive brain alerted her. Either way, she was ready when the other woman jumped at her, managing to hit Misty firmly in the face.

Misty rolled back with a groan, and Shannon stifled one of her own, having used the arm with the injured shoulder to hit her assailant. On the plus side, that probably meant she'd be able to use her arm to operate.

Several flashlights clicked on, and they all focused their beams on Misty, who sat on the floor in a miserable heap. She was sobbing at her failure, and Shannon was surprised to feel sorry for her. She still liked Misty, or at least the woman she thought Misty had been, and she wasn't unmoved by the woman's obvious misery—even if her success would've meant the end of Shannon's life. That put it in perspective, but she was still hurting for everything Misty had been through.

When Detective Silver approached, hauling her up less than gently, Shannon said, "Be careful with her."

He looked stunned. "She tried to kill you, Shannon."

"I know, Detective Silver, but she's not thinking straight. I hope medication and counseling can help her, because she's had a rough road. Just be gentle with her, okay?"

His hold loosened slightly, but he was still shaking his head as he led her away a few feet before placing handcuffs on her wrist. He started reading her the Miranda rights, but the words faded as Andre approached.

Shannon focused all of her attention on him, offering a wobbly smile. "Thank you for finding me. I guess I'm glad you were misplacing your keys a lot."

He looked stern, and his anger was obvious. "You shouldn't have done it this way, Shannon. You could've been killed. Rather than running out on me, you should've come to me, and I would have helped you."

"How did I know that? You just told me last night I wasn't allowed to leave. I figured you'd lock me up in the cabin and not do anything to save Rudy."

"There was nothing to save him from. Jared went by the house. There was no one there, but no sign of a struggle. That doesn't mean he was taken."

"He's at Disneyland. Misty knew putting him in danger would lure me out, so she texted me a picture of a knife over Rudy's head. She took it when he was asleep at the hospital a few days ago, but I didn't know that at the time. I thought it had happened today, and he was in danger."

He frowned. "That's terrifying, but you still ran off without knowing for sure. They weren't home, but that didn't mean the boy and his foster parents were in danger."

Shannon nodded. "I do understand, but I panicked as she knew I would, especially when they weren't home. She sent him and his parents away for the day so no one would know if there'd been a kidnapping."

She shook her head, marveling at the cold-blooded logic Misty must have employed to set in motion her plan. She'd spent years stoking her anger to an irrational level and fixating on Shannon as the object of her suffering. At least now she knew why her stalker had chosen her. It was a small consolation. "I'm sorry, but I couldn't risk you not helping me."

Andre reached for one of the scalpels on the table, and he didn't look at her as he knelt down to saw through the ropes binding her ankles to the chair. When he looked up finally, he seemed sad. "I can't believe you didn't trust me, or thought I would just ignore danger to Rudy. I just can't believe you risked your life without even asking for help. That was the stupidest thing you could've done."

His words were harsh, and they hurt, but they were also the truth. "I've explained to you why I wasn't certain I could trust you to help me, but you're right. This was stupid. I knew it from the start, but I did it anyway. I couldn't let her hurt Rudy. I didn't know it was her then."

He nodded before jerking his head in Misty's direction. "By the way, I recognize her fat suit. I guess that was pretty clever of her to obscure her body frame and size by adding bulk."

At Andre's comment, she looked over at Misty, whose sweatpants had slid down enough to reveal the presence of a fat suit on her frame. "She's terribly clever. She made me think I was her friend, and I never realized she hated me more than anyone in the world."

"I heard part of why," said Andre. His voice was softer now, and some of the anger had clearly drained away when he gently squeezed her uninjured shoulder. "You're right that you had no control over what your boyfriend did. The accident wasn't your fault."

Shannon sighed. "I've asked myself a million times if I could've done something different to stop him, but I don't think I could have. I was really pathetic back then, with no self-esteem. When Anthony started paying attention to me, I would have done anything he asked me to do, because I couldn't believe he liked a plain girl like me.

"I was too scared to tell him not to drive, and I figured if I stayed behind at the party, he would dump me and find someone else. I've wished over and over since then that I'd just stayed behind anyway and called the cops on him, but that's what the adult me would've done. The seventeen-year-old me was too weak to do such a thing. I could have stopped it, but I didn't. She's right about that."

Andre put his hand under her elbow and helped her to her feet, providing her plenty of support to lean against him. "You still couldn't have changed the outcome. You can't go back in time and do so, and you weren't the one driving. I understand why Misty fixated on you, wanting someone to pay for her pain, but you had no responsibility for it."

Shannon didn't bother to argue as she nodded. She would always share responsibility for the accident, because she hadn't done the right thing when she had still been a naïve teenager. It was something she deserved to carry around, but she certainly didn't deserve to die for it. "What happens to Misty now?"

"She'll be medically evaluated to see if she needs to go to the hospital before jail."

Shannon frowned at his words. "She's obviously unbalanced. She needs to be in a psych ward, not a prison."

"That takes a little time, but I'm sure that's where she'll end up. She probably won't spend time in prison for this."

Shannon let out a ragged sigh. "That's okay. I'd rather she gets the help she needs than be punished and still be broken."

"It's not like she'll be wandering the streets," called Jared over his shoulder, clearly having listened to the conversation. "She'll be held in a secure psychiatric facility until she's deemed healthy enough to be released, if she ever is. You won't have to worry about seeing her for years, if ever again."

"Thank you, Detective Silver." Shannon appreciated that he moved her more carefully than he might have other perps as he maneuvered Misty through the dark warehouse, still illuminated only by their flashlights.

Andre took her hand to lead her out, and Shannon leaned heavily against him. There was an ambulance waiting, and she didn't protest when he led her toward it. Her hands needed cleaning and bandages, and her shoulder was likely to need stitches. It might even require surgery. She clung to his hand after the paramedic directed her to lie down on a gurney. "Will you come with me to the hospital?"

"Of course I will."

"Will you stay with me?"

"Forever, Shannon." Andre's lips brushed against her cheek as he made the promise.

Epilogue

IT WAS A BIT OF A MADHOUSE, but Shannon was enjoying every minute of it. Rudy clearly was too as he sparkled as the center of attention. They were holding a party to celebrate his adoption day, and the judge had signed the papers that morning. She, Andre, and Rudy were now officially a family.

As though thinking of him and summoned him, her husband came up behind her, putting his hand on her curving belly. "How are you feeling? Is this too much for you?"

She grinned as she looked over her shoulder. "Not at all. I felt great. Not like poor Julia."

They both glanced at Julia sitting there with Justin on a patio loveseat. The wind blew through her blonde hair, and it seemed to be providing major relief for the heavily pregnant woman.

"I think I'll take her another drink. You don't think she's going to pop right here, do you?" Andre looked nonplussed at the possibility.

"No, I don't. If she was in any danger of having the baby soon, there's no way Justin would've let her travel from Montana by vehicle." At thirty-seven weeks, Julia was too pregnant to be allowed to fly, but she had been insistent on coming to the party, and it was obvious Justin couldn't deny her anything.

Shannon freely admitted her husband was the same way, but she tried not to take advantage of him. He was caring and slightly overprotective, especially now that she was pregnant, but she appreciated his care and never doubted just how much he loved her.

Or Rudy. He had been the one to suggest the adoption, but it had felt so right that she had immediately agreed. Rudy had been on board with the idea as well, and they had spent the last six months becoming a family, which culminated in the morning's legal order appointing them his parents. They had been his parents for months though. In her heart, Shannon felt like she'd been his mother since she first met him at the age of three. It had just taken her a while to recognize it.

Everything was going smoothly, and no one needed anything for the moment, so she took a seat near Rudy, putting an arm around his shoulder in a casual sign of affection that wouldn't interfere with his current interactions with the kids surrounding them. Their new neighborhood had a lot of children, and she was happy that they had accepted Rudy among them. He was thriving, and though he still had some surgeries ahead of him, and he would always have an obvious difference, she was very hopeful for his future.

Andre came to lean against her, his hand on her shoulder, and his thigh near her head. She laid against it as the wind blew in from the ocean, the sand whipped lightly around them, and sunshine poured over them. It was the perfect moment of the perfect day, and it was just the first of countless ones ahead of her with Andre and their children.

Bonus Excerpt of "Safe Harbor[1]"

---

1. https://books2read.com/u/3k0ZXG

2. https://books2read.com/u/3k0ZXG

CHAPTER ONE

JULIA BRUSHED PAST Shanae, jumping in surprise, and almost dropping the tray of drinks and empty glasses in her hand when her coworker screeched and shot away. "You sure are jumpy tonight." She sidled past the beautiful woman, wishing for about the millionth time that she had a figure like Shanae—or any of the other dancers who worked at G-Strings. "Is everything okay?"

Shanae bit her full lower lip, seeming to be on the verge of sharing something, before blinking. "Everything's fine."

She shook her head at her friend's continued stubbornness as she set the tray on the bar to load the last of the glasses that had been left behind by the patrons Tony had escorted out at closing time one hour before. "If you need to talk about something, I'm here."

Shanae gave her a shaky grin as she smoothed a hand down the dark skin of her stomach. The skimpy dancer's costume she still wore revealed the firm tautness of her muscular body. "Nah, I'd better not."

"Even if it's about Raze, I promise I won't say anything to piss you off. Or I'll try not to." Just saying Raze's name sent a slight shudder through her, and she couldn't figure out what Shanae saw in the balding, chubby, Italian man who frequented the strip club.

He'd been a regular before meeting Shanae, and he continued to come several times a week and ogle the other girls, though he was ostensibly in a relationship with Shanae. Julia tried not to be cynical, but she imagined the wads of cash Raze Marconi flashed around had a bit of something to do with Shanae's willingness to overlook his odious nature. Not that she could blame her friend for wanting security, but she wasn't at a point of desperation in her own life where she would ever consider such an arrangement, especially with someone like Raze Marconi.

Shanae let out a little gasp as she turned to face Julia under the auspices of slamming down some empty glasses onto the tray. Julia thought about admonishing her to be more careful of the glassware, but since Shanae had offered to help clean up out of the goodness of her heart, not because it was in her job description, and because she really didn't care about the glassware in the bar, she held in the reproach.

"Seriously, what's wrong? You're usually a little sensitive about him, but I've been trying to rein in any comments since you asked me to." Shanae had made it clear that Raze was a topic that was off-limits, and Julia was trying to respect that despite her disapproval of the relationship. The less she heard about Marconi, the better.

"I'm done with him. That should make you happy. Only problem is, I'm not sure he's done with me." As she said that, her gaze drifted to the door, and she bit her lip in a sign of worry.

"You think he's going to stalk you or something, or not let you end the relationship?"

Shanae shrugged. "It ain't that. I don't know how he'd feel about me breaking up with him, but as soon as he realizes what I did, he ain't going to come after me because of me ending the relationship."

A chill went through Julia at the words, and she eyed her friend with concern as she turned away from the tray of glasses and the nightly clean-up. Her attention remained focused solely on Shanae. "What did you do? More importantly, why are you afraid of him?"

There was almost a look of pity in Shanae's eyes. "You don't know who he is. Bless you for your naïveté, but you're about the only one around here who ain't got a clue."

"A clue about what?"

"Raze is in the mafia. He's like third in line for the *don* or some shit. I don't know. Alls I know is after I figured out what he's doing, I was done with him. But if he finds out..." She trailed off with a shake of her head, sending long strands of dark hair flying between the two of them. "I gotta get out of here."

Reflexively, Julia glanced at the clock. "Your shift ended forty-five minutes ago, and all the other dancers are gone. You don't have to hang around helping me out with clean-up."

Shanae shrugged. "I don't mind helping with that, but I ain't talking about leaving the club. I need to get out of the city. I gotta figure out what to do with it."

"With what?"

Once again, Shanae seemed poised on the cusp of confession, or at least conversation, but she abruptly shook her head and turned away. She pretended to busy herself with straightening bottles of alcohol, and Julia let her. It wasn't as though she could badger her friend into telling her the secrets she was hiding.

They worked in silence for the next twenty minutes, until everything was done. "I just have to close up the till, so you could head out if you'd like, Shanae."

"I'll wait for you. I was kinda hoping..."

"Hoping what?"

"Could I crash on your couch tonight? I'm getting out of town tomorrow, but I gotta get to the bank to get most of my money. I have some squirreled away on me, but it ain't enough to get far away."

"Of course you can stay, but I'd like you to tell me what's going on."

"I can't. It ain't safe, Julia. You shouldn't—"

A sound of raised voices, one of them identifiably Tony's, interrupted what she was going to say. A second later, three gunshots followed.

"Fuck, he's found me," said Shanae. "I knew I should've called in sick and just hit the road today."

"He shot Tony." Julia was sure of it as she said the words, only vaguely aware of Shanae speaking to her. She seemed to have developed a case of tunnel vision, and the world around her blurred. Her friend's voice seemed to be coming from a far distance, and she couldn't make out the words.

However, a sharp sting against her cheek whirled her back into focus, and she stared in surprise when she realized Shanae had slapped her. She understood why, since Julia had been on the verge of a panic attack. "We have to hide and call the police."

"Use the silent alarm, Julia." Shanae looked terrified, but her brain was still clearly working faster than Julia's.

With a shake of her head at her own lack of logic, she stretched under the bar and pressed the button that triggered the police to come investigate. "Now we have to hide."

There was an eerie calm about Shanae, and she stood with her back away from Julia, facing the entrance to the club. "I'm going to stall him if I can. I need you to get in my purse and take out the flash drive. It looks like a classic car. I gave it to him for his birthday, and then I borrowed it to transfer my school work for my encryption class. Fuckin' ironic, huh? There's a lot more than homework on there, and you have to keep it safe. Don't tell nobody you have it. I'll get it back from you if I can."

"What's on it?"

Shanae turned and glared at her. "Get your ass moving. Find the flash drive and hide."

Julia was reluctant to leave Shanae to face Raze, but she couldn't deny her friend's urgency, and it was suddenly contagious. She spun on her heel and raced to the back room, heading straight to Shanae's cubicle against the wall. The dancers shared a row of vanity tables, along with three large racks of costumes, but each had their own assigned personal space. Though Julia wasn't a dancer, her space was also alongside the others.

She pulled out the beige Coach bag, briefly remembering when Shanae had brought it in a few weeks ago, showing off her gift from Raze—or her newest pimp daddy, as one of the other dancers had said in a cattily way. She flipped it open and reached inside, relieved to find the flash drive at the top. She took it out and shoved the purse back into the cubicle out of habit before turning to look for a place to hide.

She wriggled into a space behind some shelves, which was fairly well obscured by one of the racks costumes, as she moved more fully to cover herself. It wasn't a very good hiding place, but was all she could do at the moment.

It wasn't a second too soon either, because almost as quickly as she had settled, two strangers she'd never seen before entered the back room. She didn't know anything about them, but judging from the way the suits stretched over their bulk, along with the discreet bulges under their left arms that suggested they carried pistols, she assumed they were some hired muscle of Raze's, if he was genuinely a mafia don.

She held her breath as they approached, certain they would somehow immediately find her hiding space. Instead, they turned their attention to the cubicles, rifling haphazardly through the belongings stacked there, including spilling Julia's purse on the floor. One of the goons kicked it to the side, sending it sliding toward her, and she almost reached out to pull it to safety before realizing what a stupid move that would be. She stifled the impulse and placed her hands over her mouth, trying to keep in any sound of fear as she pressed her hand against her lips while the other clung to the car-shaped flash drive.

One of the two dark-haired men picked up Shanae's purse and dumped it on the floor. He sorted through the things quickly with his foot before tossing aside the bag and shaking his head at the other one. "It isn't in there."

"We should tell the boss."

"Yo, Mr. Marconi, flash drive isn't in her cubicle," shouted the first one.

The other goon rubbed his ear. "I could've done that. I meant go talk to him. You didn't have to shout at him. You know how he hates that."

Before the other goon could offer a retort, Raze was suddenly in the doorway, dragging Shanae behind him.

Seeing her friend's fear increased Julia's own, and she tightened her hands even more around her mouth to keep from crying out. She felt powerless sitting there, hiding in her cubbyhole, as Shanae faced the three angry, armed men.

"I told you I don't know what you're talking about, Raze. Why are you treating me like this?" Shanae said the words in a convincing way, complete with her own dose of attitude, but her trembling lips and rapidly blinking eyes gave her away. Even Julia could see that from her obstructed view provided by a gap between two costumes hanging on the hangers.

Marconi shook her violently. "I know you took it. It was on my computer desk when I left this morning, waiting for Enzo to deliver it to the relevant party. It was gone when I got back, and you and the guys are the only ones who have access to that area of the house. It sure as fuck wasn't my old maid, who worked for my father and wiped my ass when I was a baby."

She was trying to pull off a pout, but it didn't look convincing. "Well, maybe one of your goons took it, but I didn't." She tried to tug her arm free, but ended up teetering on her high heels that she hadn't bothered to change after her last set had ended.

"Don't lie to me."

"I'm not. I didn't—"

Julia let out a small gasp, but it was quiet enough that no one seemed to hear and look her direction. What had prompted the reaction was the violent way Marconi had suddenly turned on Shanae, hands clamped around her throat. He was strangling as hard as he could, and her friend's eyes were bugging out as her fingers dug at the beefy hands wrapped around her throat. Her long acrylic nails made deep furrows in Marconi's hands, leaving blood dripping down his skin, but it clearly wasn't enough to free her.

"You don't ever lie to me. I'll find the fucking thing without you. You probably sold it to someone, didn't you, you greedy cunt?" Marconi hurled the accusations, but he didn't give her a chance to respond. He simply kept tightening his hands until Shanae's dark skin had taken on a grey cast, and her eyes looked like they were about to pop out of her skull. When he eventually let go, her body fell to the floor, and he kicked her aside as though she was a piece of garbage.

"She must've hid it somewhere. If it's not here at work, it has to be at her apartment. That's where we're headed next. We'll tear it apart, then her car. Then we'll start on the list of her friends. I want that flash drive back before it falls into the wrong hands." He paused to look down at Shanae, his disdain obvious. "You mess with the bull, and you get the horns. You thought you could blackmail me? Get a good payoff and disappear? Guess you were wrong, you whore." He kicked her body again before walking out, his goons following in his wake.

Julia remained where she was, frozen in fear, for several moments longer. She was afraid to move, just in case they were observing for any other occupants. She didn't think the thought had occurred to them though. They hadn't really bothered to search anywhere besides Shanae's cubicle. Apparently, they had assumed Shanae and Tony were the only ones left. She was never more grateful in her life to be unable to afford a car that would have betrayed the presence of a third employee in the building.

She still couldn't force herself to move away from her hiding place, but she did stretch far enough to reach her purse where one of the goons had conveniently kicked it, grabbing hold of the strap and dragging it toward her. She fumbled for her cell phone and called nine-one-one, barely managing to form a coherent sentence when the operator answered, wondering if the woman on the other end of the line got much of what she was saying as she tried to relay there had been a murder, and she wasn't certain the murderers were gone yet. She was reassured that she had pressed the silent alarm, so police would be coming whether or not the dispatcher understood her.

"IT'S NOT THE RITZ, but it'll do, I hope." Marshal Hart gave her a kind smile when he said the words as he led her into the safe house.

Julia nodded, incapable of really looking to see her surroundings. It appeared to be a bland and nondescript apartment, but it didn't matter. If she was safe, that was the all she cared about. "I'm sure it's fine, Marshal Hart."

"It's probably a step up for someone like you," said Marshal Morris Franks as he brought up the rear, closing the door behind himself and engaging the locks. "This must be like a four-star hotel."

She glared at him, resenting his attitude. Ever since he'd stepped foot onto the crime scene, answering the call from a local police officer who had seen the wisdom of involving the U.S. Marshals to protect the witness to a crime committed by a known mobster, he'd had that kind of attitude. It was clear he looked down on Shanae, the club, and Julia. "I happen to have a nice little apartment."

"Oh, really?" He pretended to be surprised, though it was obvious he was just being a jerk. "I guess dancing pays pretty well then if you have enough for an apartment after drugs and alcohol."

She put her hands on her hips, her glare deepening. "I don't have a drug or alcohol problem, and I'm not a dancer. But if I were, there'd be no shame in that. It's a paycheck. You get a paycheck for doing your job, no matter how shittily you do it. Dancers work for tips, so they actually have to be good at their job. Same with bartenders."

He scowled at her. "You sure have a superiority complex for a glorified whore."

"That's enough," said Marshal Hart in a firm voice, though it sizzled with anger. "You won't speak to any of our witnesses that way, at least not while I'm here, Franks. It doesn't matter what profession Miss

Dennings undertakes, and it doesn't matter that Ms. Hammersmith was an exotic dancer. All that matters is this woman witnessed a violent crime, and she might be able to help us finally bring down Marconi. I don't care what your own prejudiced beliefs are, but you will speak civilly to her and keep a respectful manner around our witness. Are we clear?"

Franks's lips curled upward in disgust, and his tone was far more sarcastic than subservient. "Yes, sir." He didn't bother to look at either one of them again as he moved away, muttering something about checking the security.

The agent turned to her, and the kindness in his dark eyes was enough to bring tears to hers. "Thank you, Marshal Hart."

"Call me Andre, and you're welcome. I won't let shit like that stand. I know a little something about discrimination myself, and I won't have an underling treating anyone that way while they're under my command."

She gave a tremulous smile to the African-American man, certain he must know a fair bit about discrimination. Abruptly, she realized the flash drive was still in her pocket, and she hadn't had a chance to tell anyone about it. She had shoved it there without thinking when the local police had responded to the emergency call, needing both hands to get up since her legs had gone numb from staying hidden for so long.

At first, she had been too traumatized to recall much of what had happened, and by the time the marshals had arrived, she had almost forgotten the flash drive. When she had remembered it once, Franks's disdainful attitude had been off-putting, and she'd decided not to mention it. Now, she opened her mouth to tell Andre about it, but was interrupted by Franks's return before she could do so.

"It's all clear, so you can go to bed." He phrased it more like an order than a suggestion.

If she'd been in the mood to be contrary, instead of bone-weary with exhaustion and the drop of adrenaline that left her barely standing on her feet, she would have taken a seat at the couch instead of turning to find the bathroom for a shower before going to sleep. She took a few steps before pausing to turn back to Andre. "I just realized I don't have any clothes."

"Must be a familiar state," muttered Franks quietly.

She ignored him, as did Andre. He kept his gaze on her. "If you take the first bedroom, you'll find an array of clothing for women. It should all be new. It's nothing fancy, but we keep it stocked for witnesses in just this set of circumstances. The second bedroom is for male witnesses, and the kids' room is also outfitted with supplies, in case we have families or children."

"Where do you sleep?"

"We'll take turns sharing the male witness's room," said Andre as he shot a glare at Franks, as though preemptively cutting off any kind of smartass remark. "One of us will always be awake and in the living room, or in your immediate vicinity."

She smiled. "Who's guarding me tonight?"

"That would be me, *Ms. Dennings*," said Franks in a mocking voice.

That did nothing to inspire confidence. She reminded herself Andre was there, and even if he was sleeping, he was probably trained well enough that he would respond to any threat as it emerged. Ignoring Franks completely, she whispered a good night to Andre and turned to leave the room.

The bedroom was set up as he'd promised and included a bathroom that joined to what she assumed was the other witness room. She locked both doors before taking a quick shower and sliding on a pair of pajamas that were a couple of sizes too big but were serviceable enough.

It was good they were big, because they were a little snug across her hips, but loose everywhere else. That was the story of her existence. Short and curvy, it sometimes made buying clothes difficult without trying everything on in the store. She wouldn't have that luxury here, but she couldn't care less at the moment. It didn't even matter that the waist was falling down, and she had to pull the drawstrings as tightly as she could before knotting to keep them up. Nothing mattered besides finding a few brief hours of respite in sleep.

READ MORE[1]

---

1. https://books2read.com/u/3k0ZXG

About Kit Kyndall

Kit Kyndall is the pen name *USA Today* bestselling author Kit Tunstall uses when writing steamy, erotic contemporary romances and romantic suspense. It's simply a way to separate the myriad types of stories she writes so readers know what to expect with each "author." Kit lives in Idaho with her husband, sons, and mother.

Website[2]

---

2. http://kittunstall.com/

Did you love *Hart & Soal*? Then you should read *A Royal Pain*[3] by Kit Kyndall!

A playboy prince Bennet Casparian was once a hard-partying, racing, playboy prince until he wrecked his racecar and ended up paralyzed. Now, he's wounded and angry with the world. The last thing he needs or wants is some know-it-all American pushing him to recover—especially the dowdy woman his doctor recruits for the task. But if she's so plain, why can't he stop thinking about her?**A stubborn physical therapist**Harper is happy with her job at the VA, but irresistibly tempted by her ex-fiancé's job offer to rehabilitate an injured (and spoiled) Montrovian prince. He's already driven away two physical therapists, but she's determined to stick it out.**An unexpected connection**He pushes her buttons and tries to keep her away, but she

---

3. https://books2read.com/u/3k0vvW

4. https://books2read.com/u/3k0vvW

finally breaks through his resistance. The more time she spends with him, the more she wants the prince, and the attraction is definitely mutual. Their relationship is forbidden for many reasons, so why does it feel so right?**An unforeseen consequence**They've broken the rules, and it's only a matter of time until someone finds out. When their secret comes to light, Harper might lose everything important to her—including Bennet.

9 798223 371045